WHEN I WAS BECCA GREEN

WHEN I WAS BECCA GREEN

THE TETHERED SOUL SERIES, BOOK 4

LAURA C. REDEN

When I Was Becca Green:

The Tethered Soul Series, Book 4

Copyright © 2021 by Laura C. Reden

Ebook: ISBN 978-1-954587-07-6

Paperback: ISBN 978-1-954587-10-6

Hardback: ISBN 978-1-954587-41-0

Dyslexic Edition: ISBN 978-1-954587-04-5

Cover Images:

© Adobe Stock / alexlibris

© Adobe Stock / krstrbrt

© Adobe Stock / Kevin Carden

© Adobe Stock / Stephen

© Adobe Stock / donfiore

CONTENTS

WHEN I WAS BECCA GREEN

CHAPTER 1

*H*ad I known that this would be my last life . . . I wouldn't have changed a single thing. That doesn't mean it was perfect. Not by a long shot. My time here wasn't without heartache, pain, or blood-curdling fear, but that doesn't mean it wasn't filled with pride, growth, and unconditional love. Because this life had purpose, and that's all I could ever ask for. And at the end of my days, I knew I'd earned my happily ever after . . .

It was the dead of winter, and the storm had yet to reach its peak. I was warm inside the house and comfortable enough. The medication helped to ease the pain, and though I still felt a great deal of it, the sensation paled in comparison to the emotional pain I'd felt over the years. The knowledge of that perspective was strong enough to knock a few notches off the pain chart. I did my best to hide it from Easton. He had a fire going in the fireplace, as he often did during storms like these. And he played music in the early mornings. The sweet piano notes floated through the air. They drifted down the hall until they reached my heart, placing a smile in my eyes that couldn't quite meet my lips. I wasn't sad, though—only tired. My body ached, and my sleep had been restless. I had a long day ahead of me.

I sat down at my vanity to get ready for the day. I dusted my face with powder and swiped on a bold red lip. It was a little much for the early morning, but I didn't know if I would get the chance to wear it again, and I wanted to feel pretty. It didn't look the way it used to. It settled in the cracks and crevices of my dried lips, and I knew it wouldn't be long before it bled out from under my lip line. It never stopped me from trying, though. I sighed, reaching forward and drawing in a small crystal box I kept my wedding bands in, along with a few other sentimental pieces. I pulled out the tiger's eye drop earrings and slipped them into my lobes. I wasn't as fierce as the tiger, but I liked to think I had some fight left in me. These earrings always reminded me of that.

The room flashed, and thunder cracked, sending Tiny Tommy running to cower under my seat. A small grey mop of hair found solace between the legs of my chair. "It's OK, TomTom. You're OK," I said. I reached down and picked him up. His four pounds felt like a dozen in my weak arms. His tiny frame trembled, and he licked my hand as he cuddled close. "I thought you were supposed to be *my* emotional support pet?" I sighed, looking in the mirror.

I didn't like looking into the mirror. Not because I

detested my reflection, but because I didn't recognize it. I had been aging my whole life, but at some point in time, I must have rejected it. My appearance—though Easton would tell me I was beautiful—simply wasn't me. I had always been the same girl in my core. My looks had stretched over two lifetimes. But this? This reflection was new. And I wasn't. It was a hard concept to cope with, even now, after trying for so long.

My hair was stark white and brittle. What was left of it anyway. My eyes seemed to droop, even when I was happy. Everything did. Gravity wasn't a friend of mine. My body had been losing its battle with it for seventy years. It wasn't all bad, though. If I looked closely enough—and sometimes I did—I would see the seventy years of laughter running deep in the lines around my eyes. I would see the decades of love in my cloudy, cataractous eyes. And I would be reminded of the best of times from my overworked smile in the way my cheeks hung like marionettes. It was the face of a well-lived woman, and I had earned it. I was proud of that fact, but it didn't resonate with me.

Until recently, I had felt like my youthful self trapped inside a withering body. But in the past several weeks, that had changed as well. My body hadn't been the only thing to grow weak. My thoughts were slowing down. And sometimes I felt less than capable.

I put Tiny Tommy on the floor and pulled a scarf out from within a drawer. Standing in front of the mirror, my eyes dropped from my bold red lip to my neck. I swallowed, the lump rising and falling before I covered it with my teal scarf. I tied a bow, fluffing it as much as I could to hide what lay beneath. It wasn't a secret by any means—not this time—but it didn't have to be a constant reminder.

I walked down the halls, enveloped in the piano's melody, and found Easton sipping his coffee on the porch. His grey hair swished slowly back and forth in the rocking chair as he watched the storm. Wrapping a blanket around my shoulders, I joined him, sitting in the rocker beside him. He placed a cup of coffee by my chair every single morning. It's where we had started our day for the last thirty years. This porch, that view, a cup of black coffee. I looked out to the grey sky and could barely make out the horizon. The rain pelted down between the cliffs, and it looked like we were caught in a cloud. I wondered if this was what it would be like after I passed and lived in the clouds. Though sunsets were my favorite, this storm was a sight to behold. I sipped my hot coffee and peeked over at Easton when I set my mug down between us.

His eyes were on my scarf. And though I wore it proudly, my heart sank when his gaze met mine and he nodded curtly. His lips pursed as he tried to be strong, but it was mere seconds before the tears broke from deep within. He had tried so hard to stay strong for me. Though he didn't need to. Easton's grey hair shook with his sobs, and my stomach dropped with guilt. He wrapped his arms around his chest in an attempt to stabilize himself. I lowered my gaze, and the teal scarf caught the corner of my eye, reminding me of a time in the past. A time when I desperately needed to hide behind it . . . but for different reasons than now. I pulled the blanket tight around my shoulders. It was hard to witness your best friend bend until they broke. Especially knowing that you were the reason.

CHAPTER 2

As Easton broke, I was taken back to a time when youth was upon me. When my eyes still shined and life was set at a quick and vibrant pace. It was Clara's sixth birthday party, and I was hiding in my bedroom. My heart was pounding, and my eyes wide as I stood in front of the mirror. I picked up my teal scarf, tying it every which way. Nothing I did changed the fact that I had died almost thirty years ago but was still an active member of the Clover community. I couldn't hide who I had been or who I was today. If our friendship meant what I thought it did, Lindsay would know the second she laid eyes on me. And this sheer scarf couldn't hide me from my best friend.

Easton rummaged through the bedroom, doing what he could to disguise his appearance. Hats flew over his shoulder one by one. "How's this?" Easton asked. His trusty old baseball cap was pulled down to his brow, and a pair of sunglasses blacked out his eyes completely.

"You? She's not going to recognize you!" I said scornfully.

"Perfect!" Easton spun on his heels and reached for the doorknob.

"Easton, wait!" I shouted.

"You should . . ." He hung in the balance, eyes traveling the length of my body. "You should stay here . . ."

"Stay here? How am I supposed to stay in our bedroom while I'm hosting our daughter's sixth birthday? Her entire class is out there waiting for me!" I said, running my hand through my hair.

"How are you supposed to go out there? Lindsay will recognize you. It'll be a disaster! A very *public* disaster! Could you even imagine? Just stay here. I'll tell everyone you aren't feeling well," Easton said with a quick but lasting glance of empathy before disappearing down the hallway.

I couldn't stay in our bedroom. Clara and Nora hadn't blown out their candles yet. I'd miss the whole thing. I tied the scarf around my hair, but it did nothing to shield my face. I panicked. Picking up my phone, I dialed the only person I could in a moment like this. Brooklyn. She picked up on the second try.

"Becca? Where are you?" she asked.

"Shhh. Just come to my bedroom. I need you," I hissed.

"Is everything OK?"

"No! Hurry up," I said.

I was standing in front of my mirror, trying to contour my face into a version my best friend wouldn't recognize when Brooklyn walked in. "Brooklyn, I need your help," I said, pulling her into my bedroom and closing the door behind her.

"What's going on? You're missing the party. I doubt you're going to make a good impression while you're hiding in here." Her brows furrowed as she took in my less than stellar makeup.

"It's Lindsay," I said, staring at Brooklyn's unregistering eyes.

"Who is?"

"Molly's mother is *Lindsay*!" I said through grated teeth.

"You mean Nora's mother?"

"Yes!" I hissed.

"OK. Maybe we should just call her Nora from here on out, because it's getting a little confusing . . . and . . . am I supposed to know who Lindsay is?" Brooklyn asked calmly.

I took in a deep breath. I didn't have time for back stories. "Lindsay is my best friend!" I raked my hands through my hair as I paced back and forth.

"I thought *I* was your best friend?" Brooklyn asked, one eyebrow arched.

"You are *now*! But she was *then*," I said.

"Wait, are you saying that your daughter's adopted mother"—Brooklyn placed a finger in the air, trying to connect the dots—"is your best friend . . . from your past life? *That* Lindsay?"

I felt the blood drain from my face. Seeing it with my eyes was one thing, but to hear someone repeat it back to me was a whole new revelation. Recognizing what I was up against, I took a seat on the bed, my head swimming. "Yes.

That's exactly what I'm saying. Brooklyn, I don't know what to do. You've got to help me."

"Yeah. Anything. But what can I do?" Brooklyn asked. I raised my head to meet her gaze. Neither of us knew how to remedy the situation. And even though Brooklyn had lived through some tricky times, she'd never been faced with a former loved one playing such a substantial role in a different life. I needed Lindsay to know and love me as the parent of her daughter's friend. But I couldn't have Lindsay recognize me as the girl she had grown up with—the one who had tragically died. It was more than impractical. It was impossible.

The "Happy Birthday" melody erupted in the backyard, and my eyes flicked from Brooklyn's to the window and back again. My face fell. I was missing it. I needed this to be the best birthday ever, so I would make a good impression on Nora's mother. So I could stick around for years to come. So I wouldn't miss moments like this. Like now.

"How am I ever going to be in Nora's life if I can't show my face to her mother?" I asked Brooklyn, my lip quivering.

"It's OK, Becca. We're going to find a way. I promise," Brooklyn said, pulling me in for an embrace. I fought the hug. My arms hung by my side as my head grew heavy on her shoulder. Clapping sounded from the backyard, and I wondered what each of my girls had wished for. I knew my wish.

"You should get a nose job."

I pulled away. "What?"

Brooklyn nodded in all seriousness. "Yeah. You should

get a nose job. It's perfect. Lindsay will be *reminded* of her best friend, and she'll love you. But you'll be different—just enough."

"You want me to get plastic surgery?" I asked.

"Everyone's doing it." Brooklyn shrugged.

I scowled, looking into the mirror briefly. Should I? Was that the only way? My trembling hand reached up toward my nose before I dispelled the thought with a shake of my head. Brooklyn turned to the mirror, examining her own profile.

"What if . . . what if *you* pretend to be *me*?" I said.

"What? Now, that's crazy." Brooklyn scowled.

"It's better than surgery! I mean, you just go out there and pretend to be me. How hard can it be?" It was the perfect idea. And I wouldn't have to go under the knife.

"Doesn't John know what you look like; inside and out?" A smirk spread across Brooklyn's face, and I shoved her arm—aggressively.

"Stop that!" I said. She was right though. There was a slight problem. John had been my OB-GYN. He delivered both the girls, and we had been talking for months now at school. There would be no fooling him with a stand-in.

"I don't know what to do, Brooklyn. Can you at least go get some pictures of the girls for me before it's too late?" I asked. I didn't want to be left alone in the confines of my bedroom, but a picture of my girls was something I could cherish for years to come. I hoped someone had snapped a picture of them blowing out their candles. Perhaps Lindsay had.

I sat in bed for the next hour while the party wrapped

up. Texts from Brooklyn came in one at a time. Photos of Clara with her arm around her sister. A close-up of Nora with blue cake frosting on her cheeks. And a couple of candid pictures of Lindsay. I zoomed in. The years had been kind to her. She was the same beautiful girl I had known and loved in my last life. My heart ached, knowing my best friend was so close yet so far away. I wondered what it would be like to pick up where we had left off. And it pained me knowing that we could never do such a thing.

Few families lingered behind, but it wasn't until Easton came into the bedroom to retrieve me that I knew it was safe to show myself. Nora's family had gone home, and the threat of being exposed as a Tethered Soul was finally behind us—for the time being. Though I knew more obstacles would be waiting for me in the days and weeks to come.

I helped clean up as the last of the guests parted ways. Clara didn't notice my disappearance, and I was both thankful and crushed at the same time. I threw out dozens of juice boxes and several half-eaten pieces of cake before I cut my own slice. Tanner and Brooklyn flirted in a way they hadn't in a long time, and I stole tiny glances in their direction. I watched him brush his hand against hers as they reached for the same empty soda can. Her face lit up even though she was the one who had ended their relationship. I knew she wanted what she wasn't willing to give. She feared the commitment more than the broken heart. Familiarity has a way of doing that to a person.

Easton took a seat beside me. Removing his disguise, he ruffled a hand through his hair, disheveling it. He offered a small smile, and I fed him a bite of my cake. Neither of us had to speak to know how the other was feeling. In fact, words wouldn't accurately describe it anyhow. We were caught somewhere between a curse and a gift. And it was up to us to decide which one it was going to be.

"Never thought it would be Lindsay," Easton said, ripping a napkin into minuscule pieces.

"Nope," I replied. Clara walked up to Brooklyn and asked for help to remove a doll from its packaging. I watched her struggle before taking the doll to the kitchen in pursuit of a knife. Easton followed.

"Maybe it's a good thing? At least we know Nora will be taken care of properly. Lindsay is probably a good mom, right?" he asked.

"Oh yeah. The best," I said. But that wasn't the part I was worried about. I freed the doll from its packaging and handed it to Clara. She ran away with a smile on her face. I shoveled the last bite of cake into my mouth and resolved to clean up the backyard. Easton and I talked little about it after that. And a part of me felt like my dream was over. There was only one way that I could be in Nora's life now—two if you counted the nose job. But it was risky business. And when losing the chance to have the girls grow up together was on the line, I wasn't sure I could do anything other than fold.

How would I react if my best friend came back from the dead? I played out several scenarios in which Lindsay or Brooklyn had dug out of their grave, but all of them turned into short zombie features in my head. That was the last thing I wanted Lindsay to think of me as. Forget having

Nora over for playdates if her mom thought I was of the undead race. I kicked myself for not having made some kind of pact with her. A safe word of sorts.

Later that night, when the lights were out and Easton and I lay in bed and his breathing was far too fast for slumber, I rolled onto my side, staring at him until he asked, "Can't sleep either?"

"No." A long stretch of silence passed, and had I not been watching his eyes blink, I might have thought he'd fallen asleep. "Think we're jinxed?" I asked.

"I do. I think we're plagued with having everything we wanted . . . just out of reach. I mean, you . . . our love— it just ended. Us, when we couldn't find each other. And when we did, you didn't remember." Easton winced, the pain of our reunion still fresh in his mind. "Nora, lost . . . then found. And now this. We've had everything we always wanted dangled right in front of us. What else would it be if it weren't a curse?" His forehead creased, the lines drawn from years of stress.

"I don't know . . . *luck*?" I wasn't sure why I said it. Perhaps I was just playing the devil's advocate. Maybe it was hope. But if luck had anything to do with Lindsay being the guardian of my lost daughter, I'd be forever indebted to somebody or something.

CHAPTER 3

*I*t was a particularly chilly morning the following week when Nora's nanny didn't show at drop-off. I had forgotten Clara's lunch box and was retrieving it from my truck when I spotted Lindsay walking Nora in from the parking lot. *Shit!* My heart beat thunderously as I scampered to my truck, ducking. I hid my face behind my bag, probably drawing more attention to myself than I originally would have. It was silly, really. Lindsay wasn't even looking in my direction, and I nearly had a heart attack. It was easy to see what I had been doing wasn't working. I started my ignition with shaky hands, and the second they disappeared into the school, I sped off much too fast for a twenty-five-mile school zone.

I couldn't live this way indefinitely, and actually, I was surprised I had gotten by as long as I did. That nose job was looking better by the day. With my mind a wreck, the school disappeared in my rear-view mirror. I looked beside me at a stoplight to see Clara's pink lunchbox still waiting to be delivered to the school.

"Dammit!" I hit my steering wheel, and the horn whimpered. Why couldn't it just be easy? Why couldn't Nora's mom have been anybody else? It was at times like this I felt the universe was testing me. And I was pretty sure I was failing. Miserably.

I scoured the parking lot as I came in. There were no more parents dropping children off, and I was pretty sure the coast was clear. My adrenaline was still coursing through my veins as I grabbed Clara's lunch and headed for the front office. I swung the door open, and as soon as I did, I knew I had made a terrible mistake. I stared directly at the back of Lindsay's head as she spoke with Sarra, one of the administrative staff members. The door slammed closed behind me, and I jumped. My jaw hung while I waited for Lindsay to turn around as she inevitably would. But their conversation continued seamlessly. I should have run. I told myself to. But my legs were frozen in fear. Or perhaps . . . just maybe . . . I wanted to be discovered.

"What about Tuesdays?" Sarra asked.

"I don't have a set schedule that I can come in on. I'm a nurse, and my hours rotate week by week. Can't I just pop in the morning of and ask if you need help?" Lindsay asked. Her dirty blond hair had darkened over the years, and her figure had filled out with age. I was frozen still. Afraid to stay and afraid to leave. I didn't know which would make less of a scene.

"I'm sorry, ma'am. You need to sign up on the schedule."

"But I can't commit! How can I help when I can't commit to every single Tuesday?" Lindsay's voice was elevating. She turned to glance at me, where I stood waiting behind her. "Sorry, I just . . ." She whipped her head back around when Sarra continued. I sucked in a deep breath.

"Ma'am. We need consistency for the kids. If you can't volunteer on a set schedule, then we can't have you volunteer in the classroom." A thin sheen of sweat covered my skin, and I kept my eyes trained on the floor.

"But what about parties? I saw you needed help for the class party. I think I will be available." Lindsay flipped through what I imagined was a pocket calendar.

"You need to sign up on the e-mail." Sarra's monotone never changed. If she had good days or bad days, nobody would know the difference. She was neither patient nor impatient. The only thing she ever was . . . was repetitive.

"So, I can't sign up here?" Lindsay asked, her patience wearing thin.

"Ma'am, you need to sign up—" Lindsay shook her head and threw a hand up in the air. Having heard enough, she sighed and spun around for the exit. I dipped my chin and ran a slow hand through my hair, covering most of my face the moment she looked at me.

"Can't even work for free these days without jumping through hoops," she hissed under her breath as she strode by. I sucked in a deep breath when I heard the door close behind her and I knew I was safe. I dared to look behind me, and I watched through the glass door as she walked away.

"Ma'am?" Sarra asked in the tone she wore so well.

I held up the pink lunch box. "Just dropping this off," I said.

"Drop-offs go in the bin to the left," she said, motioning behind her desk. I looked up but didn't see what she had been referring to. I smiled and began to wander. "In the bin. To the left," Sarra said once more. I startled, further embarrassing myself. Once the drop-off bin was located with no help from the staff, I left Clara's lunch and headed for the door.

Relief washed over me as the fresh air reached my lungs. I started my truck and then paused. The engine running, and my hand on the gear. I knew I should let it be, but I couldn't bring myself to drive away. I picked up my phone. My thumb hovered over Lindsay's last text message. I knew she was frustrated, and I desperately wanted to reach out. I wanted my friend back. But sending a text now would be like opening Pandora's box. I typed out a carefully thought-out message, and before I could hit send, I deleted the entire thing. I tossed my phone into my lap and pulled my gear into drive. I had no business texting Lindsay like we were friends.

The torment in my head raged on, and by the time I was halfway home, my cell phone had found its way into my hands once again. I typed out my message, eyes ticking up to the street between each word.

Hey there. I was thinking about volunteering for the class party, but I can't find the e-mail. Can you forward it to me? I don't know why they make these things so difficult!

A horn blared, and the phone fell to my feet. I whipped

my head around to see a car nearly side-swiping me and a red traffic light passing overhead. My heart hammered against my chest, and my hands trembled as I gripped the steering wheel. Reaching down toward the floorboards—careful to keep my eyes on the road—I retrieved my phone. And as safely as I could, I opened the text message I had started and hit send.

Then, to keep my mind off the line of communication I had just opened, I called Brooklyn. She was at Stanford's Coffee, and I was on my way. What I needed now was a friend. A friend that knew me and what I was going through. And probably coffee, too.

I entered the coffee shop, and Brooklyn waved me over to a table for two in the corner. A coffee was waiting for me on the table, and I smiled when I saw the foam latte heart. Inevitably, it reminded me of Lindsay and how she used to teach me latte art.

"Hey. I got you a cappuccino. How are you?" Brooklyn asked.

I lifted my bag off my shoulder and draped it across the back of my seat. "You didn't have to do that!"

"My treat." Brooklyn smiled.

"Thank you. I think I needed this. I nearly crashed my car after running a stop sign. I just can't focus lately," I said, taking a sip.

"Sounds like you need to be more careful. What's got you rattled? Is it your friend?"

I shrugged. Of course, it was, but I didn't want to bother her with all of my problems. It seemed to be one-sided lately, and I felt like an awful friend for it. "It's nothing. How are you? How are things going with Tanner?"

Brooklyn's eyes lit up. "We've been texting again. I know it doesn't mean much, but I missed it." The bridge of her nose turned pink, and the blush spread to her cheeks.

My cell phone pinged, notifying me I had an incoming text. I bit my lip. "Do you want to get back together with him?" I asked, glancing down at my bag.

"I don't know Bec. I do, but I know it's no good for either of us. He wants a family. I can't give him that." A sadness crossed her eyes as she looked around the room.

"Why not? I don't get it, Brooklyn. Why don't you give up this free spirit act and just let yourself be happy? I mean, you want him, don't you?" I asked.

"I . . . It's not that easy."

"Actually, it is. Take it from me. I did it."

"But we're not the same, you and I," she said.

"Well, I don't see why not. Have you had any dreams about it?" I asked.

"I don't have dreams about myself. It's the only thing I don't dream about."

I frowned, and my phone pinged again. This time, I reached for it, unable to resist my curiosity any longer. "Well, that has to be frustrating," I said. After reading Lindsay's text message complaining about Sarra and the school's protocol on volunteering, I cracked a smile and let out a stifled giggle.

"What's that?" Brooklyn asked.

I typed back a snarky text to Lindsay with a goofy smile on my face. "What?" I asked, my eyes glued to my phone.

"Who are you texting?"

"Oh, it's nothing." I quickly stashed my phone in my bag.

"Oh my god!" Brooklyn's jaw dropped.

The tables quickly reversed, and now I was the curious one. "What?"

"Are you having an affair with the hot doctor!?" Brooklyn cupped her mouth.

"What? No! I'm . . . I'm texting Lindsay!"

Brooklyn's face fell. "Oh," she said, with a hint of disappointment.

I rolled my eyes. "I ran into her today at school. She didn't notice me, but we've been texting," I said. My phone pinged again.

"You know that's never going to work, right?"

I sighed, knowing she was right. When I read the incoming message, it was so classically Lindsay that it made me sad. Like a little taste of a memory that I could never get back. And it reminded me of what Easton had said about everything we ever wanted being just out of reach. "I know," I said, shrugging. "Um, she's asking if Clara could go home with Nora on Friday after school. Would you be able to stand in for me and pick her up?" I asked. An unsure grin on my face.

"You want me to pretend to be you?"

"Yeah, I mean, you don't have to do much. Just be polite and pick up Clara. It's not like you have to stay and chat or anything."

"And what if John is there? He'll know I'm not you." Brooklyn's eyes searched mine.

"Well, just say you're my friend then, and that I was unavailable. Think you can do that for me?" I asked. I knew it was a big ask, but only another Tethered Soul could truly understand.

Brooklyn sighed, looking down at her coffee. "Yeah. I can do that. Better me than you," she said.

"Thank you! I'm going to text her right now," I said, typing out a reply as fast as I could. I knew it wasn't a fix for the future, but it was a decent patch for the time being. And I was excited that the girls could hang out again.

That Friday, Clara was thrilled to be going home with Nora after school. I hadn't been to the Faye's house before and I was curious to hear every last detail from Brooklyn. When Lindsay texted me their home address, I immediately made plans for a drive-by in the near future. I exchanged a few texts between Lindsay and Brooklyn during the day regarding pick-up. And when the evening came, I had pizza ready for dinner as I waited impatiently for Brooklyn to arrive with Clara. I ate breadsticks while staring at the front door. And when a car pulled into my driveway and headlights brightened my windows, I rushed to the front door.

"Mommy!" Clara ran into my arms.

"Hi, baby! How are you?"

"Good. I had so much fun!" she said.

"You did?"

"Yeah! I want to go again!"

"Hey," Brooklyn said, with wide, telling eyes, and I immediately knew that my plan hadn't played out as seamlessly as I hoped.

"Oh no. What happened?" I asked. Brooklyn stepped inside, and we both peered down the hall to make sure the little ears were out of earshot.

"So, I went to pick up—"

"Was their house nice?" I asked.

"Yes. Focus," Brooklyn said.

"Right. Sorry."

"And Lindsay opened the door. She shook my hand and said, 'You must be Becca, it's so nice to meet you,' or something like that. And I just smiled and shook her hand. She didn't think twice, and she invited me in while Clara gathered her things." Brooklyn spoke fast and quietly.

"OK. Good. There's pizza here, by the way," I said. Brooklyn glanced at the pizza and ultimately grabbed a slice. "Go on." I encouraged her.

"So then, she said, 'I ended up volunteering at the class party. I was surprised I didn't see you there,' and then I said, 'Volunteering isn't my thing,' and she gave me this weird look, and things went sideways from there."

"Oh no! You didn't!" I said.

"What?"

"I told her I wanted to volunteer for that party," I said, placing my forehead in my hand. "She thinks I'm a total flake now."

"Well, if she didn't then, she definitely did when John rounded the corner and she found out I was an imposter!" Brooklyn said nonchalantly.

"What!?" I grabbed hold of my head, making sure it wouldn't spin around completely.

"Yeah. He said, 'Who's this?' And Lindsay was like,

'What do you mean? It's Clara's mom,' and he was all, 'Um, no. It's not actually—'" Brooklyn made her best male doctor's impression.

"Holy shit. Please stop! This is unbearable!" I said, standing up from the dining table and pacing the length of the small kitchen. Before today, my chances of watching Nora grow up were slim, but now that they thought I was lying about who I was, it was nearly impossible. I might as well say goodbye to Nora all over again.

"It's fine. I mean, I don't think it was *that* bad."

"What do you mean?" I asked.

"Well, I just explained to them that you were busy, so I was helping out." Brooklyn shrugged it off.

"But you said that you were me?" I asked.

"No! No. Technically, I didn't say that. It's not our fault that Lindsay interpreted it that way," she said with arched brows.

I came to sit down beside her at the table. "Brooklyn, I'm so screwed," I said, my forehead resting on the table.

"Hey, I did the best I could under the circumstances," she said.

"I know. Thank you. I'm not saying any of this is your fault. It's not. It's my fault." I looked up at Brooklyn and forced a smile. ". . . I should have just gotten a nose job."

Brooklyn giggled just as Clara reached the table. The three of us picked at pizza for dinner while Easton worked late. And it wasn't long before two of my favorite people in the entire world made me forget all my problems. However, it was long after Brooklyn had gone home and Clara was down for the night that I lay in bed thinking about all the worst possible scenarios that may come from baring my face to my former best friend, and now, the mother of my child.

Any way I sliced it, the risk was exponential. What if she thought I had faked my own death? What kind of person would do that? If Lindsay didn't believe me or, worse, thought I was driven by dark forces, I'd lose Nora all over again. But, if Lindsay accepted me, I'd lose my tether, and this would be my last life with Easton. It was no surprise that my only two options made me sad. The stakes were high in each likely outcome. But there was only one thing driving me now, and that was to protect my girls. And I was willing to give up my immortality if it meant I could do so. My mind was set. I'd confront Lindsay, and I would tell her everything, whether or not she was open to hearing it.

CHAPTER 4

It took nearly two weeks before I could get Clara a playdate with Nora. Lindsay had been slow responding to my text messages, and I was convinced that John had a cold shoulder at pickup. I knew the stunt I pulled with Brooklyn was bad news, but it was clear after the following weeks that it was worse than I imagined. I tried to explain, but it didn't translate well. On this particular evening, both Easton and John were working late. I used it as an excuse to have a glass of wine with Lindsay after our kids played. I must have practiced what I'd say to her a dozen times. None of it was right. I'd have to wing it, and I had never been good at that.

The bottle of wine had nearly slipped out of my sweaty palm just before I rang the doorbell. Her house was beautiful. Massive compared to mine. Rose bushes lined the walkway leading up to decorative double steel front doors. A blurred figure approached as I watched through the glass behind the steel. The small security camera in the corner hadn't gone unnoticed, and I knew there was no turning back now that I'd been on camera. The ominous dusk sent chills down my spine as the figure approached and I heard the footsteps. Was it Lindsay? Her nanny? I kept my sunglasses on so I wouldn't startle her before my entry. If there was one small goal that I had for today, it was to make it past the threshold. The knob turned as a lump stuck in my throat. This was either the stupidest thing I had ever done in my life or the bravest and most courageous act of love I could think of. Either way, I was about to pass out.

The door opened, and Lindsay smiled before me. She had a casual air about her. Jeans and a T-shirt, twisted leather sandals. She waved me in, and I could see her brows pull together as she assessed me for the first time. Her house was beautiful from what I could see, but dark through the lenses of my sunglasses.

"Hi, it's so nice to finally meet you. I brought some wine; I hope you like red," I said, my head spinning.

"Oh, yeah, I do. Thank you," Lindsay said, taking the wine from my sweaty grasp. "Come on in." I wiped my palms on the legs of my jeans as I followed her through the house. I passed by photos on the foyer table and pulled my glasses down to the bridge of my nose, glancing as I passed by. A grand vase of fresh tulips dressed her dining table. It looked like something out of a magazine. I folded my glasses in my shaky hands and sucked in a broken breath of air before we reached the kitchen. A large granite island with a farmer's sink graced the center of the room. French doors opened up to a patio fountain, and the trickling sounds of water helped ease some of my anxiety. Lindsay busied herself fetching wine glasses from the cabinet as I set my things down on the countertop slowly. I stood meekly in the corner, arms crossed over my chest as I waited for the shrill that was about to come.

"We're still settling in, so sorry for the clutter. It's just been so hectic around here with work and school . . ." Lindsay said, opening the wine. The house was meticulous. Not a box in sight. I came to her side, timid and slow as a cat on the prowl. Lindsay smiled, her eyes finally lifting to mine as she held out my glass of wine. The stem slipped from her hand, and her smile shifted from poised to panic. And right before it came crashing down, and red wine surged everywhere, I thought I saw a hint of grief. That look . . . that horrified look, like all the pain of the day I passed had flooded back for just one second.

Wine spattered everywhere, and the glass scattered across the floor. "Oh, god! I'm so sorry!" Lindsay said, immediately bending down to pick up the broken pieces of glass. I looked down at her; my jeans stained with wine. She murmured something inaudible, shaking her head in distress. I lowered, slowly. My eyes focused on her.

"I don't know what's gotten into me," she said.

I took a deep breath and reached for a broken piece of glass by my feet. "I do," I said. Lindsay deliberately raised her gaze to meet mine. Our eyes connected, hers in inquiry. A moment passed as wonder traveled through her eyes. Then she was on her feet. Quickly, she spooked. Taking a few steps back. Her mouth gaped, and her hand, full of broken glass, began to tremble.

"Mommy!" Clara shouted.

Both Lindsay and I shouted back. "Glass! Careful, there's glass!" It was all it took before the girls giggled and took off running in the opposite direction. My eyes flickered between Clara's back as she disappeared down the hall, to Lindsay's face of utter disbelief. Both of our arms outstretched to keep the girls away. Silence stretched between us, but I had no words to make this any easier.

"I . . . I'm sorry. I . . . It's just, you look like someone I used to know," Lindsay said. She laid the glass down on the table behind her and dusted off her hands. Her eyes filled with hurt. I could only imagine what it was like for her to lose me. If I had lost her, nearly thirty years ago, I would be beside myself. Would it be easier for her if I were back? Would it be better that she could talk to me again? Was this a gift of friendship?

I cleared my throat yet spoke softly. "Everly," I said, in a knowing tone.

What passed through Lindsay's face was unrecognizable to me, but the single tear that rolled down her cheek was no mystery to either of us. "How did you know that? Who are you?" The sorrow melted away with the hint of conspiracy.

I took a step forward, the glass crunching under my shoes. Lindsay took a step back. She was afraid of me. I dropped my gaze to the puddle of wine beneath my feet. I often wondered how I had ended up in this mess. And this very moment was no different.

"It was nearly thirty years ago. I had cancer. I was terminal," I started. Lindsay grabbed her stomach and started heaving. I started for her but then stopped myself the moment she cowered. I stood at a distance as she worked through it. I wasn't sure she was listening, but I continued anyway.

"I didn't want to tell you. I was afraid our friendship would change. I was afraid you would pity me. And that was the last thing I needed. Not just from you, but from anyone," I said. Lindsay spun around. She staggered out of the kitchen, her hand grasping at the wall for support. I followed her, keeping my distance. I needed her to hear me. And I needed to say it now before I was no longer allowed in her house.

"I was afraid of dying, but I was even more afraid of change!" Lindsay grabbed the back side of her sofa, her knees faltering just before she went down. "Lindsay!" I lunged to her side. I patted her cheeks, and her head wobbled ever so slightly. She was out cold. I surveyed the room for help. John was working late tonight. The girls must have been playing outside. "Lindsay?" I asked, patting her cheek some more.

She moaned, twisting her head and wincing. She reached up to grab the back of her head as her eyes parted. Just as I came in to focus, she screamed. Eyes wide with horror, she scooched back on the floor, gaining as much distance from me as she could. I glanced around, worried the girls might be alarmed.

"You! You!" she stammered.

"Lindsay! It's me! I'm not going to hurt you!" I said. She rose to her feet, but her legs were wobbly as she shifted her weight from side to side. "You should really sit down. Can I help you sit down?" I motioned to the sofa.

Though Lindsay looked at me with fear in her eyes, she did what I said. Slowly, she made her way to the sofa. I reached out to support her elbow, and she yanked it away, glowering at me. I held both hands up in the air like a white flag if I ever had one. "There, do you need anything? Can I get you some water?" I asked, glancing back at the kitchen.

"Wine. You can get the wine," she said. I nodded and rose to my feet. "Bourbon! Get the bourbon . . ." Lindsay pointed to a cabinet across the room. I rummaged through the countless bottles of hard alcohol before I found the bourbon. Shot glasses were on the side of the cabinet, and I placed two on top of a cutting board that was adorned with limes. I slowly walked back to Lindsay, careful not to spill on my already stained jeans. She took hers, knocking it back before grasping for my shot, too. It looks like I'd have to do this sober.

"You're not Beck. It can't be. It doesn't make any sense." She took another sip of her amber shot. Her eyes unfocused before her.

"Easton was easy to love," I continued. "He was the only one who understood me in a time I didn't know myself. He knew things, too. He knew about the path I was on. How unfortunate I was. How it felt to have a death sentence. He knew what I was going through . . . and he knew what I was up against. Because he had done it all before."

"Done what before?"

"Died," I said.

Lindsay's gaze lifted to meet mine. "He'd died before. Many times."

"No. No, this doesn't happen," she protested, her mind clamping down on what she had known to be real for all these years.

"His soul . . . it was immortal. No matter how many times his body died, he would come back to do it all over again. I don't know how. I don't know why. He said it was a curse." I hunched over my crossed arms as I sat opposite from Lindsay. I felt the need to reach out to her, but she was too far away.

"So what happened to you then? They said you died. I went to your funeral." Lindsay knocked back the rest of her shot, and the girls ran by the window outside. I watched them with fear in my heart. I truly hoped this wouldn't be the last time Clara could play with her sister. I had to choose my words carefully.

"Easton became my only support. I pushed him away. But I needed him. The day I gave into him was . . . well, I don't remember much, but it was the best choice I had ever made for myself. I wanted to marry him. Even if it was for a short while. I wanted him to know that he was the love of my life. And I had little to give in my final months. So, I gave him my hand in marriage. It was beautiful. It was private. And I knew that my parents were throwing a reception for us when we got back. It was supposed to be a surprise, but I had overheard them planning it one morning. I knew you were there when the cops showed up."

"How? How did you know? They said you died!"

"I did. It was my fault. I . . . I distracted Easton from the road. It was raining, and he swerved into oncoming traffic. The car went over the bridge." My voice trailed off into the distance. It was the one memory I kept clear as day. The one I wished I could forget. "We drowned," I said in no more than a whisper.

Lindsay cupped her mouth. Any conspiracy she had thought of me had temporarily been dwarfed by compassion and empathy for her former friend. "You drowned . . ." she repeated.

"We survived the crash. It took me a little while before I came to, but when I did, my seatbelt was jammed. The doors wouldn't open. And Easton wouldn't leave my side. We didn't die from the crash, we drowned in the river. After it happened, I saw everything. I saw the past and present. I saw the future. And then . . . and then, I did it all over again. Same soul, same body. Different family, different life."

Lindsay sniffled and swiped a tear from her cheek. She fetched another two shots of bourbon, but this time, she offered one of them to me. "And you . . . you just . . . what? Started over?" Lindsay evaluated me, head to toe, as she counted out the years on her fingers. Her face flushed when she realized this was no tall tale.

"Yeah, I did. I just started over. I didn't think a thing of it. I had no memory. Just an unfounded and irrational fear of the water. And if I'm being honest, when I look back, there were some nightmares, too."

"How are you here? Now?" Lindsay asked, confused in her own right. I didn't expect this to be easy for her to understand. It was impossible, after all. I didn't know what kind of world I was living in, but it wasn't the one I had always known to be true.

"It's a long story. But I guess the short answer is . . . fate?"

CHAPTER 5

Lindsay sat coiled on the sofa, hugging a shot glass filled to the brim with warm, silky bourbon. She stared at me sideways, waiting to call my bluff, when the doorbell rang.

"Pizza!" Nora screamed. Clara rounded the corner after her sister as they barreled toward the front door. Lindsay pulled her gaze from mine, looking over her shoulder at me before disappearing into the foyer. I closed my eyes and took in a deep breath as I slouched against her deep-seated sofa, expanding my lungs until they hurt. I ran my hands through my hair and looked around. Dusk had given way to nightfall, and it was dark outside. I made my way to the kitchen and began to clean the spilled wine with paper towels. I could hear the girls make their way to the dining room. Shortly thereafter, Lindsay came into the kitchen to fetch plates.

"Oh, you don't have to clean that," she said.

"It's OK. I don't mind." Lindsay grabbed the broom and

swept. Neither of us spoke, though I imagined her mind was anything but quiet. With the two of us working together, the mess was cleaned up in no time. We joined the girls at the dining table for dinner. Lindsay stole sideways glances at me in between the fragmented conversation and bites of piping hot pizza. Every time I caught her questioning eyes peeking in my direction, my stomach would drop with frightening speed.

"So, John is working late tonight?" I asked, even though I already heard he was. It was the very reason I had picked tonight to have wine. I couldn't have had him here while Lindsay melted down.

"Yes. And he was your doctor, correct?" she asked, trying to put the pieces together.

"Yes! He was. Small world, huh?" But Lindsay only stared at me with a deep crease in her forehead. "Um. Girls?" I pried my eyes from Lindsay's suspicious eyes. "Did you know that?" I asked.

"What?"

"That Nora's dad was the doctor that delivered . . . Clara?" I said, nearly faltering in the end.

"What?" The girls giggled.

"It's true!" I laughed with them, though my laughter was rooted in nervousness, not humor. Lindsay's eyes softened, but she was far from laughter. "Nora's dad was the first one to hold Clara as a baby. I remember the day like it was yesterday. He handed her to me and announced that she was a baby girl—"

"You thought I was a boy?" Clara asked, and Nora laughed.

"I didn't know what you were. I didn't find out beforehand."

"Why?" she asked.

"Well, that's a good question. And one I don't have an answer for. I guess I thought it would be fun to have a surprise. Like being surprised on your birthday. You know what I mean?" I asked.

Clara nodded, deep in thought. "Mom, did Dad deliver me, too?" Nora asked. My heart lurched and I let out a forceful cough. It pained me to hear her ask. A girl should know where she came from, and Nora did not. And neither did her mom.

"No, honey. I had a different doctor," Lindsay said.

"Why?" Nora asked.

"Um, because, it's standard practice to not have personal relationships with your doctor."

"Why?"

"Because it can cloud judgment, honey. Now eat your pizza," Lindsay said, her eyes shifty. Only I had known the real answer. And I could now tell that Lindsay was uncomfortable for more reasons than one. She had never told Nora that she was adopted.

When the girls finished their pizza, Clara asked if we could stay a little longer. I glanced at Lindsay, assessing her capacity for my presence. But when I couldn't get a gauge on it, I told Clara we could stay for just a bit longer while I helped clean up. The girls squealed as they scampered off, leaving dirty plates and half-eaten crust in their wake. I smiled apologetically at Lindsay as I picked up after the girls.

"If you really are Beck, then where did we work together?" Lindsay asked, narrowing her eyes.

"Easy! Fresh Grounds! You always had the best latte art. Mine was a muddled mess," I said, remembering the days when Easton would walk into the coffee shop and my heart would be set ablaze.

"When did we meet?" she asked. Brows raised.

"Come on. The sixth grade." I shrugged. If she was testing me, she would have to try harder than that.

"What teacher?"

"Mr. Richio," I said with confidence.

Lindsay stared at me, unblinking. "Anyone could have known that." She shrugged.

"Try me again?" I dared her.

"OK. Who was my first kiss?" Lindsay asked, squaring off with me as she popped a hand on her hip. A smile spread across my lips because this was a game I knew I would win. And this was something she had never told another soul. Something she had barely confided in me in the first place. And something I couldn't forget.

"Grant Stevenson!" I pointed my finger at her chest. Her eyes rounded and the thin, straight line of her lips softened. "He was your first kiss. It was in second grade, and you kissed behind the slide. He told everyone, and you denied it for years. He turned into a giant nerd, and you were his only claim to fame. You were so afraid that if anyone found out he'd been your first kiss, your reputation would go down in flames!" I pointed.

The best part was seeing her finally crack, giving in to

everything we both wanted but were so afraid to reach out and take. Our friendship.

"And you know what the funny part is? He's totally hot now!" I said. Lindsay laughed, and I chuckled. "It's true! I saw a picture of him online!" The internet was a mysterious world, both wonderful and overly invasive at the same time.

"How do you know that? I never told anyone that!" Lindsay said, wiping her eyes.

"You told me. And I remember it because that's the kind of thing a best friend keeps locked up tight." I shrugged. Our eyes locked onto one another's, and she smiled at me, not completely understanding but accepting nonetheless. "I remember. It's me. I'm here," I said, wrapping my arms around her and burying my head into her shoulder. I cried when I felt her slowly reciprocate, embracing me.

"I've missed you so much!" Lindsay cried.

"I've never stopped thinking about you!" I confessed.

"Never!" she agreed.

"You've always meant so much to me! I love you so much! I should have told you more often! I'm sorry. I'm so sorry!" I bawled. All the stress that had built from the moment I laid eyes on Lindsay at the girls' birthday party had peaked and now was spilling out as I sobbed on her shoulder.

"No, I'm sorry! I love you, too!" We stood there in the kitchen. Two friends reuniting. Thirty years after one's early departure. And it was like no time had lapsed at all. We weren't kindred spirits like Clara and Nora but similar in an unexplainable way.

The hours flew by. Both Clara and Nora fell asleep during a movie while Lindsay and I rehashed old times. Her memory was far better than mine. She told me how she and John had met. And how she swore she had recognized Easton at the coffee shop, and then again at the house. She told me about my Pop—which I had known—and then she told me about my mom.

"I work at Sunny Hill Assisted Living. Your mom is a patient there. She has dementia. I've been taking good care of her."

"My mom has dementia?"

"Yeah. It's bad. She no longer remembers who I am." Lindsay scratched her head, deep in thought. "Maybe you should visit her?" she asked after some time.

"Really? You think?" I asked.

"Well, I mean, if she doesn't remember you . . . maybe it's kind of . . . perfect? In a way..." Lindsay said with empathy-filled eyes.

"Yeah. I guess you're right. Would you be able to get me in?" I asked.

"Absolutely! Just say you're a volunteer, and I'll sneak you onto the schedule. Let me know whenever you want to come in, and I'll have you directed to her room, even if I'm not there. But, if you are going to come, I would probably plan it soon. I'm not sure how much longer she has," she said. I nodded, remembering the time I said goodbye to my pop. It didn't end well.

My phone buzzed. A text message from Easton. "It's late. I should probably get going."

"Yeah. I'll walk you out."

I scooped up Clara's limp body and walked her out to the car. I buckled her in and shut the door before turning to Lindsay. "I'm going to see you again, right?" I asked, worried that she would wake in the morning with regret.

"I mean. I would like that. Would you like that?" she asked.

"I just want us to go back to how we were, before . . ." I shrugged. Lindsay chuckled.

"We're not kids anymore. Have you seen my hair?" she joked.

"I mean, like the way things *should* have been."

"Yeah, only you've still got your youth," she teased.

"But you can overlook that, right?" I asked.

"Look, I can overlook your youth if you can overlook my grays. Deal?"

It was a deal I couldn't pass up.

"Deal," I said. I gave her a hug and told her I loved her. And we planned to meet up the following day at Sunny Hill. Overall, it went better than I could have hoped for. I had my friend back, and things were looking up. There was only one small piece of information I hadn't disclosed. And that was because I was sure it would send Lindsay scaling the walls. Surely, she would put as much distance between me and my family as possible if I told her I had not only come back from the dead but claimed my stake on her daughter, too.

Secrets were terrible to keep. The weight heavy upon my back. I had carried so many of them throughout the years, I'd learned they often weren't worth it. But that didn't keep me from withholding the truth. There was an art to timing, and I knew that the timing wasn't right with this particular secret. Lindsay had a lot to unpack after our talk, and I needed her to trust that my heart was pure. I didn't want to take Nora from her, even though I wanted nothing more than to have her under my roof. I'd still be honored if I could watch her grow up under Lindsay's wing. She was doing a fine job. And I was content with that.

Easton helped me unload Clara from the car. She slept peacefully in his arms and slipped into bed without ever waking. As soon as her door was closed, he turned to me in question. "How did it go?"

"Well, at first, not great. I think I ruined my favorite jeans," I said.

Easton looked down at my thighs. "Then?"

"Well, then she fainted and started knocking back shots of bourbon."

Easton looked at me sharply. "I'm afraid to ask what happened next," he said, brows furrowed.

"Then she believed me! And we're friends again!" I said, a gigantic smile plastered on my face. Easton cracked a grin and pulled me into his chest.

"Oh, I'm so happy. I really needed that win," he groaned.

"Long day at work?" I asked.

"Long, long day."

"Well, I might be able to help with that?" I pulled away from his grasp and unbuttoned his top button. The desire to celebrate the turn of events flickered inside me.

His eyes gleamed down on me, and his hands responded by running the length of my body. I unbuttoned three more buttons before spreading his shirt opened and planting kisses on his chest. His hand wrapped around the nape of my neck as he pulled me in, kissing me deeply. I closed my eyes and let the stress roll off me in waves, crashing at my feet.

I pulled away for a breath, biting his lower lip gently, and our eyes caught just before he grabbed me and threw me over his shoulder in one swift motion. I screamed in delight and clapped a hand over my mouth, afraid to wake Clara. Easton ran down the hall as I muffled my wails of laughter in my hands. He nearly decapitated me with the door frame when he spun around to close the door behind us. I screamed again. Then, I was falling onto the bed. I braced myself as Easton jumped on top of me, silencing my squeals with his kisses and unwinding my anxious body until I longed for the night's sleep.

CHAPTER 6

I checked the directions on my phone one last time, making sure I was headed in the right direction. It didn't seem like a road that an assisted living home would be down, but I drove slowly, checking the signs anyhow. When I came upon one that said Sunny Hill Assisted Living, I pulled in and found a parking spot. It was sad to think that my mom had ended up here after losing her daughter and husband. And I wondered how often my brother visited her with the kids.

The live-in facility smelled like a mixture of hospital antiseptic and crocheted blankets. A small gathering of seniors sat quietly in an open game room to the left. None of them spoke, and none of them were watching the TV. I bit my lip as I approached the front desk, worried about what state I would find my mother in, and worse yet, if she would recognize me.

"Hello. Um, is Lindsay Faye working today?" I asked,

playing with the collar of my shirt. Even though it hadn't been tight, it felt somewhat restricting.

"One moment." The lady picked up the phone and spoke softly into the receiver. "She will be out shortly. You're welcome to take a seat," she said, with an open palm. I saw the few chairs lined against a wall and smiled before sitting. I clutched my bag in my lap, wringing out the straps. I didn't know why I felt so nervous. If my mom couldn't recognize Lindsay, and she was in the late stages of dementia, surely she wouldn't recognize me. Especially after not seeing me for thirty years.

Lindsay and I had been on good terms when I left her house the night before, and I doubted that she'd reconsidered in such a short time. I rubbed my arms, though I was anything but cold. It was an uncomfortable feeling knowing I, too, could end up in a place like this. Or more like a *state* like this. I knew a little bit about what it was like to have memories escape you. And I knew enough that I didn't want to experience slowly forgetting my loved ones. To watch them hurting, having no control over it.

"Beck!" Lindsay rounded the corner with open arms.

"Hi!" I stood, giving her an anxious hug.

"I still can't believe it!" she whispered in my ear.

"I know. I'm sorry," I said. I never wanted to be a burden on anyone, and I could tell by the way she was looking at me that I'd rocked her world. Everything she knew to be true had been obliterated when I walked through her door just the night before.

"I was up all night! Just thinking about it." She shook

her head, staring at me like it was the first time. Like we hadn't just had a full night of disbelief.

"I know it can be a lot to take in. I didn't sleep well either," I said, thinking back to how torn up my bed had been in the morning's light. I tried to hide the coy smile that wanted nothing more than to spread its wings.

"Well, we can talk more about it later. I'm sure this isn't the place. Why don't I show you to your mom's room, and then we can chat before you need to take off," Lindsay said.

"That sounds great." I nodded, and my memory of being tangled up in Easton faded away. I followed Lindsay, taking multiple twists and turns until we reached one room in particular that made my stomach flutter.

"Are you ready?" she asked.

"I think so?"

"Just be patient with her," she said, opening the door. "Good morning, Mrs. Beck. I brought a friend with me today. I hope you don't mind. This is . . ." Lindsay looked at me, stumbling over her words and prompting me to answer. But all I could see was a woman who resembled my mom.

She was smaller than I remembered, but that may have been the way her back hunched. A dark green duster covered her shoulders, and her hair was fluffed in a way she'd never worn it before. She looked at me, her face etched with the years of heartache, and she . . . she looked right through me. Not an ounce of recognition. No eternal bond that was strong enough to pull her mind from the depths of deterioration. Nothing but an empty gaze. And I loved her all the same.

"Uh, uh, Becca," I said. Staring.

"This is Becca." Lindsay turned to me, and whispered, "Just text if you need anything. I'll be available all day." She clapped my shoulder as she passed by. I nodded. Quiet blanketed the tiny room, and I startled when the door clicked shut behind me. My heart floundered in my chest, and I didn't know what to say or do. I wrung my clammy hands and cracked several knuckles, buying myself time. Then, I took a step toward the woman I used to call Mom. My mouth felt dry. The words I had practiced earlier had vanished entirely and were replaced with an unfortunate melody in my head.

I couldn't for the life of me understand why this would happen to somebody. She had already lost me. And no parent should have to experience that. But then she had lost my dad too. She'd lived alone for years thereafter. And as if she hadn't lost enough, now she had lost her memory? It didn't make any sense at all. *Why* would this happen? *How* could this happen?

I pulled up a chair and took a seat next to my mother. Her hair was thin. Her skin so lean, it was translucent. Her eyes, yellow. She looked . . . sad. She looked caged within her body. A body that no longer served her. She looked . . . *Tethered.* Had this been what Easton had felt like all these years? Like his soul had outgrown its body? Like he'd been ready to move on but couldn't? Trapped?

There was a muffled knock. Must have been the room next door. I listened to the muted conversation and then the laughter. Joy spread through the walls and out of the vents when I was sure nothing could penetrate them. I looked up to the vent in the wall and smiled at the vitality next door. Mom did, too.

She only smiled, but it was enough to get me through the fear of seeing her current state of mind. At least now, I knew she was capable of joy, and that not all had been robbed of her. It wasn't long before there was a knock on our door, and I met Tommy. He was a therapy dog, a beautiful black lab. He smiled just as much as my mom did. His jowls hung as he panted big heavy breaths. He was polite in the way he held back his wet slobbery kisses. Mom clapped her hands ever so softly—a habit she had picked up from Chloe. I used to hate when she did it. Now, it touched my heart.

Tommy's wet nose bumped her face, and she lit up. Her body shook with laughter as she stroked his back, giving him as much love as she could within her brief window of Tommy time. "This is amazing," I said. "Do all the residents respond like this?" I asked Tommy's caretaker, a middle-aged man with dark skin, soft eyes, and scrubs adorned with hotdogs.

"Most do. It's really something to see how they come alive with a furry friend," he said.

"How often do you come?" I asked.

"We come once a week," he smiled.

It seemed scant. Why didn't the facility have its own live-in therapy pet? "Wow. Can't you come more often? Like every day?" I asked.

"That would be wonderful. But we just aren't capable of that right now. Hopefully, one day we will grow, but it's a small mom-and-pop shop. And there is only one Tommy," he said. I looked over to my mom, completely connected with this dog, when moments before I hadn't realized that she could engage at all. His tail slapped the backs of my knees with excited energy. And I wondered if I, too, could get a Tommy. What was stopping me from having a service dog? I could bring joy to all the residents here, and I could do it daily. Why should they have to wait a whole week? My mind raced with the possibilities.

"OK, Mrs. Faye, we need to go, but we'll see you next week," he said. Mom gave Tommy one last hug before he jumped off her bed and down to the ground.

"Um, do you have a business card? I'd like more information," I said.

"I don't carry business cards, but I can give you Lisa's phone number. She's the owner, and she would be happy to answer any of your questions."

"That would be great," I said, taking out my phone and entering Lisa's number.

When Tommy left, the letdown was immediate. Mom was quiet, her eyes plunging through gloom before landing on vacancy once again. I had seen others walking through a garden when I came in and texted Lindsay to see if that was something we could do. I imagined getting some fresh air and sunlight would be good for my mom and her mood. When I got the green light, I helped Mom put her shoes on. They were more like house slippers than anything else. She leaned heavily on me as I slipped them on. She was more than willing to go with me on the adventure, but her gate was no faster than a crawl. At this rate, it would be nightfall by the time we made it to the garden and back again.

Things moved a lot faster once I secured a wheelchair. It had been abandoned in the hallway, and I assumed it was for situations like this. I sat her down and took her for a spin outside. Her face lit up, but nothing compared to when she saw Tommy, which hadn't been anything like when she saw me. I lowered a red rose to her nose, and she smelled it with a slight curvature in the corner of her smile. I knew I wasn't supposed to, but I picked it. The gardens must have taken so long to maintain, and the flowers were meant for everyone to enjoy, not take. But roses were my mom's favorite, and I wanted nothing more than to get her smile back. I was breaking the last couple of thorns off the stem when I heard footsteps come up behind me.

"You know you're not supposed to pick the flowers, right?"

I turned to see Lindsay. My heart kicked some extra beets. "Oops. No, I didn't know that. I'm sorry," I said, shrugging. I gave the thornless rose to Mom, and she took it with a slow, trembling hand.

"So how's it going?" Lindsay asked.

I took a deep breath. I didn't know how to answer honestly. And I was still in the presence of my mother, whether she was following our conversation or not. "Good," I said, my pitch high and sharp.

"Oh, no. What's wrong?"

I sighed. Even after three decades of absence, she still knew when I was lying. "Nothing, it's just . . . she doesn't recognize me." It came out before I knew that it'd been what bothered me the most.

"But that's a good thing, right?" Lindsay asked.

I shrugged. "I guess so. I just didn't expect it to hurt like this." I tightened my grip on the wheelchair's handles, forcing it over a lump in the grass as we strolled through the garden.

"I know. It's hard for me too, and I see it every day. I see the family members come in with trepidation and leave with disappointment. Eventually, many of them stop coming. And that's the worst. That's when the patients usually start to decline, and they do so pretty rapidly. So, it seems like they don't notice, but they do . . . in their own way," she said, sitting on a stone bench by the fountain. I parked Mom beside us and took a seat next to Lindsay. "You know, that's going to be us one day," she said.

"I know. I think about it all the time. You'll have to tell me what it's like," I said, smirking.

"Oh, come on!" Lindsay shook her head. "I'm old enough to be your mother," she said, exasperated. And it was true. She was.

"Yeah. In this lifetime," I agreed, looking at my mom's paper-thin hands. Lindsay bumped my shoulder with hers, and I forced a small smile. I didn't want to feel like this. Like I was helpless. Like I was a victim of whatever life threw my way. "Hey, are you going to the rain forest play at school next Friday?" I asked.

"I'm going to try to make it. I'm scheduled to work the night shift, but I think I can get off an hour early. My co-worker said she could cover for me. John's hoping to be there, too. Nora has been fretting over her lines all week."

"What part does she play?" I asked.

"She's the snake."

"Clara is the humming bird. I'm happy to help them learn their lines. They could practice together this week?" I asked, checking my watch. Time had been creeping up on me, and I would have to leave soon to get Clara from school.

"That would be great."

"OK. Good. Well, I should get going," I said.

"Yeah, it's about pickup time, huh? I'll bring your mom back in and get her settled. It's movie night tonight," Lindsay said, standing.

"OK. Thanks." I bent over, giving my mom a hug and a kiss on the cheek. Her hands never leaving the rose in her lap. "I love you," I whispered in her ear.

I pulled away to see the same distant gaze in her yellowing eyes that I had seen most of the day. I was hoping she would give me the same warm glow she gave to the service dog, but it wasn't even close. My love had simply gone unregistered. The lifetime of memories, gone with the wind. Never to resurface again.

I sighed and forced a smile for Lindsay. I didn't want her to see just how naïve I had been about my mother's condition. As I drove to the school, I tried to focus on the positive—though there had been little of it. Even so, my mom's dementia was the only reason I could visit her, and a small part of me wondered if it was fate twisting in its mysterious ways.

$\mathcal{E}$aston had the day off. He didn't get them often, so picking Clara up from school was something new and exciting for him. But nobody could be more thrilled than Clara herself. She wanted to show her dad off to her new friends at school. I was excited too because I was going to a therapy animal center with Brooklyn. The drive was two hours with no traffic, but I intended to hit some traffic on the way home. I wasn't going to buy a dog, even though I'd come to want one since meeting Tommy. But today, I planned to start my research by asking questions in person. And a few friendly pats on the head were always welcome if the opportunity presented itself.

The facility was a little difficult to find. Tucked behind an industrial park sat the small run-down animal center. "Is this it?" Brooklyn asked.

"I think so."

"Do they train the dogs here?"

I browsed the lot, looking for life. "I don't know. It looks a little small. Let's go find out," I said. We entered the center and found not a single soul. The front desk was bare, and the chair sat empty. "Hello?" I called out.

"Hit the bell," Brooklyn whispered. I looked down on the counter, and tucked behind several flyers was a small silver bell. I tapped it twice. When it was clear that nobody was coming, Brooklyn and I began to roam the property. She slipped her hand into the crook of my arm, and we explored the premises at will. The hall gave way to multiple kennels. Only a couple of them had dogs. One was a lively boy, sure to alert the owners that they had company. The other was an older dog. His black fur hid his sad face, and he lay motionless on the floor.

"Awe. What's wrong with him?" I asked.

"I don't know. Is he sleeping? I think he's sleeping."

"He wouldn't be sleeping through all this commotion. I think he's sick," I said.

"Maybe he just needs a home . . ." Brooklyn gave me puppy dog eyes of her own, and I slapped her shoulder. She wanted me to get a dog, too. And together, we were a terrible combination.

"Stop that. I'm not getting a dog. I haven't even talked to Easton about it."

"He knows you're here though, right?" she asked.

"Yeah, but he thinks I'm looking into working with the therapy dogs. Not bringing one home. I can't just come home with a dog," I said, mostly for my own ears to hear.

"What's that one's deal? Aren't they supposed to be

calming?" Brooklyn pointed to the golden retriever, who hadn't stopped barking since we walked into the kennel.

"Can I help you?"

Brooklyn and I jumped. I spun around to see a middle-aged woman with short curly hair and a stained smock.

"Hi. Um, I rang the bell up front, but nobody answered. I'm sorry . . . I just wanted to speak with someone about the therapy dogs?" I asked, twisting my fingers into knots.

"Are you here to pick up?" the woman asked.

Brooklyn elbowed me in the side. "Oh, no. I was just going to ask some questions. You see, my mom is in a nursing home, and I'd really like to get more service dogs to visit the residents. And since that won't happen on its own, I was thinking maybe I could get involved. Maybe I could bring a service dog to visit? I wasn't really sure how it all worked," I rambled.

"I see. Well, my name is Sandy, and we have a new litter on the ground now. They're out back. This yellow guy is completing his training next month, and he's already been purchased," she said, pointing to the kennel.

"What about him?" Brooklyn motioned to the other dog.

"Him? Oh, he's not for sale. He's deaf."

"Oh, got it." Brooklyn nodded.

"But why isn't he for sale?" I asked, not wanting to give up on him just yet.

The lady shrugged. "Well, nobody has ever wanted him. He's been with us for years. It would take a really special person to take care of him. And he can't get fully certified because of his hearing. Do you girls want to see the puppies, though? They're a real hoot!" she kicked her thumb over her shoulder.

"Puppies!" Brooklyn said as she blew past me. Sandy led the way, and my eyes fixed on the deaf dog as we passed his kennel. The closer we got, the louder the puppies became. And as soon as Sandy opened the door, five little ankle biters rushed to our feet, licking, nipping, and tripping over themselves. "Can I pick one up?" Brooklyn asked.

"Sure. I've been wrestling with these guys all morning. I'm sure they could use some fresh blood. Have at it," Sandy said.

Brooklyn chose a curly-haired black and brown one to hold first. But before we left, I knew she would hold them all. Brooklyn was an animal lover; she always had been. But she had a rule about that too. "Love them and leave them," she'd always say. Something about getting the best of both worlds. Snuggles and kisses without picking up after them.

I never thought about it until that moment, but it was more of a life mantra than a rule that applied to pets. As I watched her—eyes squinted and mouth puckered as she tried to escape the direct contact of a tiny tongue—I realized she was the very same way with Tanner. She clearly loved him, but she wouldn't allow herself the commitment. She was always one foot out the door. At the least, I felt blessed she had never been that way with our friendship.

I kneeled down, and paws pranced upon my thighs, climbing me like an obstacle course. I did my best to pet them all, but their appetite for attention was voracious.

Brooklyn and I giggled when one pup turned feisty. Its growl wasn't yet fierce, and its size was anything but powerful. Still, the little bundle of curly hair continued to call out one of its brothers or sisters to a duel. They remained unaffected.

"Do you see it?" Brooklyn whispered. I looked around the small fenced-off yard. Several training stations. Food and water. Sandy.

"See what?" I asked. But she simply motioned to the surrounding air with a soft smile. I looked up, and though I couldn't see the love like she had, I smiled, knowing it was there. Sometimes I would see it, but I guessed that most of the time, I did not. My sight wasn't as strong as Brooklyn's or Easton's, and I couldn't see all the emotion and energy that they had described to me. I took another look, letting my eyes lose their focus just above the playing puppies, but nothing came into sight. It never did when I tried.

Sandy let us play with the puppies for quite some time, and when she got tired of watching us, she went inside for coffee. I glanced over at Brooklyn, who wasn't slowing down in the least. I knew she could play with these critters for hours. I on the other hand . . . I couldn't stop thinking about the deaf dog that slept through our arrival. "I'm going to go talk to Sandy. Did you want to stay here?" I asked Brooklyn.

"Do you have to ask?" she replied.

I chuckled. It was the exact response I had expected. I headed inside and found Sandy at her desk with a mug of piping hot coffee. The steam rose under her nose, and she blew on it before taking the tiniest of sips, careful not to burn herself.

"Hey, Sandy? I was wondering if I could spend a little time with the black dog." I motioned back towards his kennel.

"Bodie. Yeah, we can go see him." Sandy put her coffee down and took me to see the dog with the buried eyes. "Deaf dogs get startled easily. Here's a little trick I use to wake him up," Sandy said, getting down on her hands and knees. Bodie lay sound asleep, just like he had been when we arrived. Then, Sandy took a deep breath and blew on his face. The air ruffled his bangs, and his paws twitched in response. A smile spread across my face as she tried again. This time more air. Bodie's nose flared and his brows lifted. His eyes were partially visible for the first time. Finally, he wagged his tail, slapping it on the ground. Sandy got to her feet and opened the kennel door.

Bodie sat up, taking me in. "Hi! Hi! What a good boy you are!" I cooed.

"Now, remember, he can't hear you," Sandy said.

"Oh!" I stopped to give Sandy a look of regret. I wasn't sure how to talk to a dog who couldn't hear me, and I was embarrassed for not thinking it through.

"It doesn't mean you can't talk to him. Go ahead if that's what you want to do. But you can't give him verbal commands. They have to be visual." I nodded, brows furrowed.

But when I turned back to Bodie, and his hidden black eyes, I did it again. "That's a good boy!" I said, under my breath. His mouth parted, and he panted, opening his enormous mouth and displaying his sharp teeth. "Is he trained to be a therapy dog?" I asked.

"Well, yes and no. He is, but he has restrictions. Most of the therapy relies on sight and smell. But he is at a disadvantage without his hearing. If someone were to fall or call for help, Bodie wouldn't know unless he was within proximity to see it happen," Sandy said, leaning up against the wall.

"Could he visit a nursing home?" I asked.

Sandy sighed. It was clear she thought Bodie was a lost cause, but I wasn't giving up on him just yet. "Yes. He's fit for an ESA."

"An ESA?" I asked.

"An emotional support animal," she said. I turned to Bodie, petting his fluffy head, and I swore he smiled at me.

Brooklyn wandered down the hall, her face pink from the mid-morning heat. "I thought I would find you here," she said.

"This is Bodie," I said. His tail slapped the ground as he looked up at her with his big black eyes.

"He's perfect. How much?" she asked. Surprise sparked in Sandy's eyes.

"Look, he's not for everyone—"

"I'm not everyone!" I said, hopeful.

"Well, he seems to like you. Let me talk to my husband. If you want to leave your information with me, I can get back to you. But are you sure you don't want a pup? They will be fully trained in under two years—"

"Two years?" I interrupted.

"Yes, but—"

"How much will a fully trained pup cost?" Brooklyn asked.

"... $8,500.00 with full training, but—"

"Wow," I said. I had no idea they would cost so much. I only wanted a dog to make my mom happy. Put a smile on her face more often than once a week. I scratched behind Bodie's ear. "Sorry, guy," I whispered, knowing he couldn't hear me but that maybe he could sense my expression.

Saying goodbye to Bodie was difficult. I hated to think of him sitting in that kennel alone because of his deficit. But I left with Sandy's card, and she promised to speak with her husband regarding Bodie's fit for someone like me.

"Can you believe how much they cost?" Brooklyn asked when we reached the truck.

"I had no idea. Why can't I just bring any old dog into the home? As long as they're nice, I don't see why they need to have special training."

"Maybe you can?" Brooklyn shrugged.

"I'll have to ask Lindsay," I said. Then, I started the truck and pulled out onto the main road.

"About that . . ."

"What?" I glanced over to Brooklyn. Her face marked with guilt. "What did you do?" I asked, reluctantly.

"I may or may not have led you to believe that revealing yourself to Lindsay was a bad idea. It wasn't. It never was. And I knew all along. I'm sorry," she said.

"What!?" My jaw dropped, and I scowled at Brooklyn beside me for as long as I could keep my eyes off the main road. "Why would you do that to me? I spent weeks hiding from her! It tore me apart, and you knew that!" I barked.

Weeks had passed since the birthday party where I hid in my truck at pickup, fearful I'd lose Nora all over again. Every time I confided in Brooklyn, she would urge me not to show myself to Lindsay. She never said it outright, but she hinted at it being a mistake. One that I wouldn't be able to take back.

"I know! I know! I had a dream—"

"You said you *didn't* have a dream about it!" I said.

"I lied. I'm sorry. I'm telling you now. What else can I do, Bec?" she said, her face wrapped in defense, but her words apologetic.

I sighed. I was infuriated by her choice, but she was right. What else could she do but come clean now? I had already told Lindsay everything. "Well, are you going to tell me about the dream, or?"

"Well, don't be mad at me!"

"I *am* mad, Brooklyn. That's my right. OK? You don't know how much I worried about that. Should I tell her? Should I not? Will I lose Nora? And it all could have been prevented if you had just told me what you dreamed about. So, will you just tell me what you know?" I pulled onto the highway.

"I had a dream. There wasn't much to it. But you and Lindsay were best friends again. You were happy. The kids were happy. Everyone lived happily ever after! Is that what you wanted to hear?" she said, annoyed.

I should have been relieved. My life was complete. Job well done. I'd been successful at raising a happy family. But I couldn't understand why that had been a bad thing. And why Brooklyn's disturbance had overshadowed the bit about living happily ever after. "So, what's the problem, Brooklyn? What am I missing here?"

Even more frustrated now, she said, "Me! You're missing me! Where do I fit into this perfect life? If I'm not your best friend anymore, and you don't need me? If I'm not Tanner's girlfriend? Then I'm just a wanderer. Again. Then, this life has been another waste!" her voice wavered in a moment of weakness.

"Brooklyn! What are you talking about? You're always going to be my best friend!"

"But what about Lindsay?" she asked.

What about Lindsay? She had been a pillar in my life since I was young. "Why don't I get both? Why can't I have a best friend from each lifetime?" I asked.

It made little sense until I considered her insecurities. "Look, you can't compare our relationship with one that I have with someone else. That's not fair to you or me. You did that when I got married to Easton, too. And you're doing it now. I'm starting to think that your problem isn't insecurity within our own relationship but within yourself. Maybe you see me getting close to other people, and it makes you realize you're not doing that for yourself! And maybe you should be!" I said, stealing a quick glance at her while I drove. I couldn't see much, but I could tell that her jaw had been clenched tight by the hallows in her cheeks. "Does that sound right?" I asked.

Brooklyn stared out the window, her frustration keeping her from speaking.

"Brooklyn? Could you be mad at yourself for not committing to Tanner? Maybe that's why you're putting so much pressure on our friendship to carry you through? Maybe that's why you don't want me to be friends with Lindsay?"

She took a long while to mull it over in her head, chewing her cheek and fighting back tears. And when she finally opened back up, all she could say was, "Tanner's seeing someone else."

CHAPTER 8

$\mathcal{I}$t was the following day when Easton texted me from work saying that we'd have company for dinner. Tanner was coming over with his new girlfriend. She was someone he'd met at the Decord Police Station. Of course, I wanted to meet the girl that could be my sister-in-law, but a part of me felt disloyal to Brooklyn for doing so.

I promised myself I wouldn't make the same mistake twice, though. When my brother brought home his girlfriend and announced that he was engaged, I'd hated his fiancée. Chloe was completely wrong for my brother. And of course, I had already picked out the perfect girl for him. It took me quite some time to realize I had been wrong, but it wasn't until a lifetime later that I realized just how wrong I had been.

Not until I saw Chloe at the park did it resonate with me that love wasn't a choice. If it had been, Carter would probably have made the obvious choice. A sweet girl that everyone liked, and one that he got along with well. But his heart chose Chloe instead, and it was hard for me to see why. Eventually, I made peace with the fact that their relationship was meant for them to feel, not for me to see. And I didn't want to make assumptions about Tanner's relationship in the same way, just because I had picked Brooklyn for him instead of whomever he was to bring over.

I spent the day preparing lasagna, breadsticks, and salad. I cleaned the house and still managed to take Clara to the park for a half-hour. I had just placed fresh flowers on the dining table when I heard a knock on the door.

"Your uncle's here!" I announced to Clara.

"Uncle Tanner!" Clara wailed, running down the hall.

Normally, Tanner would let himself in, but he must have been trying to be polite in front of his new girlfriend. I opened the door, Clara by my side. Tanner was dressed a little nicer than normal, and his hair was done for the first time in a long while. His girlfriend was a cute girl. My guess was that she was a redhead by nature, with the dusting of freckles over her nose and cheeks. But as she stood on my doorstep, her hair was a dark chocolate brown. Eyes blue, and skin fair. "Hello!" I said.

Tanner introduced us. "Becca, this is Charlie. Charlie, Becca."

I shook Charlie's hand and welcomed them inside. Tanner picked up Clara and threw her into the air. She squealed, free-falling until he caught her again. A pink hue crossed Charlie's cheeks as she beamed up at Tanner and my daughter, and I could see the appeal he had on women.

He was handsome, fun-loving, and a terrific uncle. "Can I get you something to drink?" I asked.

"Oh, I brought wine," Charlie said.

"Perfect!" I took the bottle, uncorked it, and poured two glasses. I knew Tanner would want a beer, so I pulled one from the refrigerator as well.

"Thanks. Where's Easton?" Tanner asked, taking a sip of beer.

"He should be here any minute," I said, checking my watch.

"Come see my doll house!" Clara said, pulling on Charlie's jacket. Her eyes flickered between me and Tanner before agreeing.

"Oh! Here, take this!" I said, holding out the glass of wine. She smiled and took it with her to Clara's room. "You're going to need it," I mumbled under my breath. If I knew my daughter, I knew she would keep her busy for hours, and at some point, I would have to rescue her. But for now, Clara could show Charlie her room, and Tanner and I could chat, privately.

"So?" I asked Tanner, wagging my brows.

"So, what?" he played dumb.

"So . . . tell me everything! How's it going? How long have you been seeing her? Oh . . . is this your first date? Tell me this isn't your first date?" I asked, leaning across the kitchen counter.

Tanner pulled out a barstool and took a seat on the other side. He rolled his eyes at first, but then dove in more than willingly. "It is. I mean, we've had lunch together at the station, but we've never gone out before. Can you tell? Is it obvious?"

". . . And you brought her *here*?" My neck craned at the absurd thought of a romantic first date being spent in my daughter's bedroom. *Alone.*

"Well, I thought it would make her more comfortable since she knows Easton and all." Tanner nodded his head, proud of his considerate ways. Still, he was missing the mark.

I didn't want to crush him, so I didn't remind him that his new girlfriend was playing dolls in a bedroom with a six-year-old instead of being swept off her feet. "I see . . . You're so thoughtful," I said.

"I don't want this to be weird between us because Brooklyn is your friend and all," Tanner said, one cheek lifting into a forced, empathetic smile.

"Oh, no. Please don't worry about that. I've already committed to having an open mind. And all I really want is for you to be happy. I mean, I want Brooklyn to be happy too, of course—"

"Of course—"

"But, it's separate. They're two different relationships, and honestly, they're not mine. So have at it," I rambled.

"So, you're OK with this?" he asked.

"Yeah! Of course," I said, my face warming under the lie of it all. I *was* OK with it. I was happy for him. But that didn't mean I couldn't also feel guilty—like I was doing something wrong by having her over for dinner. Like I had helped Tanner fall for another girl, despite my friend being in love with him. But he didn't need to know all that. I raised my wine glass to my lips and let it linger before drawing in a long, tart sip. "Do you love her?" I asked.

"Charlie?" Tanner flinched.

"No, Brooklyn . . ." I whispered, craning my neck to peer down the hall.

Tanner looked over his shoulder, then lowered his voice. "Bec, you know I can't."

"I know."

"She doesn't want me. I was ready to give up having a family for her, but if she doesn't want to marry me, regardless of having a family, then what's the point?" Tanner said, resting his chin in the palm of his hand, hopeless.

I only wished Brooklyn could see she had choices. That her life wasn't black and white the way she always made it to be. "I love Brooklyn. You know that, but if she can't get out of her own way, she can't expect you to wait around," I said, shrugging. It wasn't the way I wanted it to be. But I was ready to accept it. Tanner already had. "Charlie seems nice though," I said.

"She is. She's got a real sweet temperament too. Everyone really enjoys being around her at the station."

"Good. That's good. You need a nice girl. Speaking of, I guess I should go rescue her from Clara, now."

Tanner smiled. "Yeah, and put in a good word for me while you're at it."

I raised my eyebrows as I passed by, but I never made it down the hall. The doorbell rang just as I left the kitchen. I was shocked to see Lindsay standing on the other side of the door; a bottle of wine in her hand and an apologetic look on her face.

"Lindsay! Is everything OK?" I asked. Her hands twisted nervously over the neck of the bottle.

"Yeah! I'm so sorry for coming by unexpectedly, but I wanted to talk to you about something. Do you have time?" she asked, peeking inside. I didn't. But I couldn't turn her down. She needed me, and it had been a long time since that happened.

"Yes, come in! Come in!" I said, waving her inside. "This is Easton's brother, Tanner."

Tanner shot from his seat and shook Lindsay's hand. "Hello," he said.

"And his girlfriend, Charlie, is playing with Clara in the bedroom," I said, worry warming my cheeks. It had surpassed the time I was going to allow Clara to steal our guest of honor away.

"I'll go keep her company," Tanner said with a smile, taking out another beer from the fridge. "You two can talk."

I laughed because playing dolls was hard work, and sometimes a glass of wine or a can of beer helped bring out the creativity. Tanner was quick to learn, as he had played dolls a time or two before. I mouthed "Thank you" to him and patted his shoulder as he passed by.

"I actually have a bottle open if you want some of this one?" I held the bottle of red wine up, trying to read the label, but it was in French, so I didn't try to pronounce it aloud.

"Perfect," Lindsay said. She sat down where Tanner had been, and I poured her a glass of wine. "I know you have guests. I'm so sorry. I just . . . I'm having a hard time believing you're back. So, forgive me for popping by. I just wanted to see you in person. I should have called. And—"

"No, no, no. Don't apologize. You can stop by anytime! OK?" I gave Lindsay her glass of wine.

"And . . . I have a proposition for you," Lindsay said, dipping her chin into her chest.

"Huh. Why does this sound like a bad thing?" I asked.

"No! It's not! Unless . . ."

"Unless, what?"

"Unless you don't want to do it, and then you feel like you need to because I asked." Concern spread across her face and settled in the lines of her forehead.

"OK. Just ask. You're making me nervous."

"OK, I'm sorry. Well . . . you know Penny? My nanny?"

"Yeah. I mean, I know *of* her."

"Well, we caught her stealing, and I had to let her go today."

"No way! What? How?" I stammered. The thought of a thief watching Nora made my stomach twist.

"We have nanny cams around the house. They're these little cameras you can hide in plants or stuffed animals. Wherever really. We caught her on one of those. I had been suspecting it for a little while now, so I set up the camera in my bedroom where I keep my jewelry." Lindsay sighed.

"She stole your jewelry?"

"No, that's the funny part. She bypassed the jewelry and stole some of my perfume. Go figure." Lindsay shrugged.

"Yeah. Huh. Maybe she thought the jewelry would be too obvious?"

"Yeah, maybe?"

"Well, I'm glad you caught her. I know you have gone through a couple of nannies, though, so that's hard," I said.

"Well . . . that's the thing . . ." Lindsay took a long swig of wine and looked anywhere but at me.

"What's the thing?"

"I was wondering if maybe, *you*, wanted to do it?" Lindsay asked, her face scrunched with worry.

"Me?"

"We would pay you! But it's not because I think you need the money or anything! I mean, I know you don't have a job right now . . . Not like that means you're looking, or that staying at home is bad, or—"

"Lindsay, stop! Stop! I'll do it," I said.

"You will?"

"Yes. I love Nora. I love you. I'm happy to help in any way I can," I said. And she didn't know how true that statement was. I hadn't yet told Lindsay that Nora was of my flesh and blood. But even if she hadn't been, I would have loved her for being my best friend's child.

Lindsay nearly knocked the barstool over as she jumped from her chair and gave me a tight hug. The back of my throat burned, and I told myself not to cry. This was the best news I could have received. I had the privilege of being in Nora's everyday life? Everything was falling into place.

"I love you, too, Everly." My stomach dropped. It was the first I'd heard my name in a long time. It sounded foreign but still pulled at my heart strings. I blotted the corners of my eyes.

When Lindsay pulled away, she too was misty-eyed. We

both chuckled at each other. She took a seat and pulled out a folded-up piece of paper from her bag. A schedule. As it turned out, Nora was a busy girl. She had school, dance, and piano. I took the piece of paper from Lindsay and studied it.

"Is it too much?" she asked.

"Oh, no. That's not it. I was just thinking, I should probably enroll Clara into the dance class too if I'm going to be there anyway," I said. "I think she'll like that."

"Um, so . . . sometimes we work the night shifts. And by that, I mean a lot of times we work the night shifts."

"OK," I said, nodding.

"Usually, Penny would stay the night at our house. She was a partial live-in."

"Oh?" I hadn't known that.

"Yeah, but since you have a family, maybe Nora could stay here some nights? I'm trying to change my schedule to the day shifts. I'll take a pay cut, but I think it will work out nicely because one of my co-workers is saving for a house, and I think she wants to switch schedules . . ." Lindsay shrugged. "Anyway, I think the sleepovers will only be for the first two or three weeks, and then the schedule will be normalized. Are you sure you're OK with this?" she asked.

"Of course. Anything you need." And I meant that. I'd do anything she needed me to do.

"I owe you. I can't thank you enough!" Lindsay placed her hand across her chest and took a sigh of relief. I smiled, knowing that I was of help to her. But nothing was better than knowing we would spend more time with Nora.

I could hear that Tanner was growing bored when his

voice boomed through the walls. "Oh, how rude of me. I forgot you have guests. I'll be on my way." I checked my watch. Easton was more than an hour late to dinner. Worry spread in the pit of my stomach as I reached for my phone to text him. I had a missed call from a number I didn't recognize. Lindsay stood and gathered her things. I held up a finger while I checked my voice mail.

I felt the blood drain from my face the moment the recording began referencing a local hospital.

"Is everything OK?" Lindsay whispered.

I sucked in a deep breath. "It's Easton," I said, my voice shaky and small.

"Easton?"

"Tanner!" I yelled. He came barreling down the hall wearing a pink princess crown and gobs of makeup.

"It's Easton. He's in the hospital!" Goosebumps prickled my skin. Lindsay gasped. I turned to her. "Watch Clara?" I asked, squeezing her forearm.

"Yes. Absolutely."

"I'll text you as soon as I know anything," I said, grabbing my keys and purse as I ran toward the door.

"I'll drive," Tanner said. I gave him a quick nod and headed for his police car parked in our driveway.

CHAPTER 9

Tanner drove like a bat out of hell. His driving put Everly's to shame, but the flashing lights and piercing siren made it not only acceptable but normal. We were weaving in and out of traffic so fast that other drivers couldn't lay eyes on us, which was a good thing because if they had, we would have struck them as crazy people. I had been so worried about Easton that I hardly noticed the clown faces on both Tanner and Charlie. Or the pink tutu tucked just under Charlie's armpits. But for those out there that weren't petrified to lose the love of their lives, I'd imagine that two pretty pink princesses driving a cop car screaming down the highway was quite a sight.

I couldn't think of Tanner and Charlie, though. And honestly, I couldn't think of Easton either. What if he didn't make it? What if he died, never having seen his girls grow up? What if he left me behind? What then? My mind raced to places it had never been before and places it never wanted to see. Thankfully, it wasn't long before I was on my feet again. Charlie and I on the flank of Tanner. He ran with one hand on top of his head, securing the plastic tiara in place. The emergency doors slid open as the three of us ran to the front desk.

"Decord P.D. My partner's just been admitted. Easton Green," Tanner said, flashing his badge. The receptionist's eyes grew to the size of saucers before falling back to her computer screen. She must have seen a lot come through those hospital doors, but I imagined this was a first. My heart raged in my chest, and I thought for a moment that I might pass out. My hands trembled and knees wobbled. I was going to be sick to my stomach. Tanner shot Charlie a weary glance. One that I wasn't supposed to see but did.

The receptionist told us to have a seat. She said that someone would be out shortly with an update. At least, that's the gist of what I understood. The fear that coursed through my veins did little for my cognitive function. When Charlie headed for the waiting room, Tanner nudged my arm, beckoning me to follow. Without his cue, I may have stood there alone, frozen in worry, still waiting for instructions.

Even though I followed Charlie to the waiting room, I didn't sit with her. I paced back and forth, biting my nails mindlessly until shards of pain would light up a nerve. Only then would I shove my hands into the back pockets of my jeans before taking them out and chewing on a new nail. I jolted every time I saw a person walk into the waiting room, hoping it would be Easton's update.

But they were families like us, coming to wait for news that may change their lives. Maybe it would just be for the night. A missed date or no time to study for a test the following morning. They'd be the lucky ones. Because as I looked around the waiting room, I knew that the inconvenience for some would pale in comparison to others. Some might spend their time teaching their loved ones to walk again. Some might lose their chance to have their father walk them down the aisle. Or a chance to tuck their child into bed at night.

A young boy, maybe six or seven, was curled up on his mother's lap, asleep. They'd probably been here for hours. Across from them was an older couple, presumably husband and wife. They held hands and shared the same worried look on their faces. And in the corner sat a woman all by her lonesome. Her foot bobbed as she scrolled through her phone much too fast to know what she was looking at. They were all similar. Loved ones, sick with worry. Waiting.

A middle-aged man dressed in blue scrubs walked into the waiting room, and everyone craned their necks hopefully. My heart stopped until the doctor spoke. "Carmichael?" he called. The mother and son perked up, and the rest of them fell back in their seats. My shoulders fell, and I turned away from the doctor, giving them an ounce of privacy. I glanced over my shoulder as the mother and son followed the doctor into the nearby hall. I wondered when I would get an update on Easton. It shouldn't be taking this long. Why was it taking this long? I took out my cell phone to text Lindsay that we were at the hospital waiting for an update when I heard a blood-curdling scream.

My back went rigid, my thumbs froze on top of my cell phone, the text message coming to a halt. Just beyond the corner where the waiting room met the hall, the mother had sunk to her knees. The little boy patted her head as she sobbed—uncontrollable and erratic cries of grief. My stomach dropped. I had heard the cries of loss before when they escaped my own mouth. They were unlike anything else I had ever heard. It's a guttural cry and sounds nothing like the pain of a broken bone or a cut knee. Saved for a time when your heart leaves your body and searches for a loved one that is no longer there.

I watched as the doctor kneeled down, cupping her shoulder. It did nothing to console her. Nothing would now, except time itself. My heart ached for the little boy who hadn't yet understood how his life would be forever changed. All he knew now lay in front of him, and that was his mother, broken in pieces. The heartbreak spread like a virus, and I could see it in the faces of the elderly couple and the lone woman. My eyes met Tanner's, and it was evident that he, too, had been startled by the woman's cries. I switched hands, biting into a fresh nail.

"Green?" a doctor called out.

"Yes!" I waved frantically. Tanner and Charlie sprung to their feet. And as the doctor flipped through his chart and began the update, all I could think was how happy I was that he hadn't called us into the hallway.

"Easton is currently in surgery. He's been shot in the abdomen. We couldn't save his kidney and had to remove it. You've got a couple of hours before he is out of surgery, moved to another room, and can have visitors. You're welcome to stay here and wait . . ." The doctor's eyes traveled from Tanner's tiara to Charlie's tutu. "Or, you can go home and return when he is ready for visitors if that meets your needs," he said.

"No. No. I'll be right here. Waiting," I said, taking a moment to catch my breath. "He'll be alright, won't he?" I asked, reaching out and grabbing the doctor's arm.

"Oh yes. You can live a good long life on one kidney," he said, smiling.

I turned to Tanner and buried my head in his chest. I don't know why I cried. Relief, I suppose. I didn't know what I'd do without Easton by my side. I wasn't the mother I knew I could be, and he helped fill in the gaps where I could be stronger. He put a light inside me that made me whole. Without him, I'd be my worst self. And he . . . he'd be starting over again. Cast out into this world like a fish released back to sea. I'd spent my whole life looking for him, and I wasn't convinced I'd be as lucky as I was my second time around. Or even my first, for that matter.

By the time I gathered myself enough to pull away from Tanner's arms, the doctor was long gone. Charlie stood awkwardly, stroking my back. I gave her an apologetic smile as I wiped away my tears. "Why don't you two get going? You must be hungry. We never ate dinner," I said.

"Oh, no . . . we're OK," Charlie glanced up to Tanner, unsure.

"Um, maybe I should take Charlie home. Then I'll come back?" Tanner asked.

"Honestly, I don't mind," she said. The three of us stood there for a moment, undecided. Until Charlie chased away the silence. "Here, I should give this back to you before Tanner takes me home," she said, tugging on the tutu. She pulled it down, but it was far too tight to get over her chest.

"Here, let me help you," Tanner said, taking the pink gauzy ruffles and trying to pull it down. It didn't budge.

"Maybe go up?" she asked.

"Let's go up," he said. He tried to lift it over her head. One quick tug and it breached her shoulders. The crack of the band ripping as it caught under her nose. "Oops!" Tanner froze. Charlie was stuck with her arms high in the air, and she glared with embarrassment through the holes in the gauze.

"Don't stop! Help me!" she hissed.

Tanner looked at me, "Sorry Becca, I'll have to get Clara a new one," he said.

"It's OK. Help her!" I waved him on, quickly glancing around to see how much of a spectacle we'd made. He ripped the tutu in half, freeing Charlie from the confines of the skirt—and the embarrassment. Her pink lipstick had smeared under her nose where the skirt had caught. Tanner handed me the shreds, and I balled them up in my hands.

"I'll be back as soon as I can," he said.

"It was nice meeting you. I'm sorry this wasn't the night you had in mind," I said to Charlie.

She took me in her arms and squeezed me tightly. "Please let me know if you need anything. I can help. I want to help," she said. I smiled warmly at her. It was then that she won my heart. I knew she'd be good for Tanner, and I was happy for him. I patted him on the back as the two of them left the waiting room with pink lipstick spread halfway to their ears. Matching purple eyeshadow and fake eyelashes glued right beneath their eyebrows.

"Wait!" I called out, just before they disappeared beyond the automatic doors. They turned around with concern. I ran to them, pulling out my cell phone. "I want a picture," I said.

Tanner's head fell back, and his eyes rolled up. The tiara fell off his head, and he bent over to pick it up off the ground. But when I held my cellphone up to take a picture, they both plastered on a forced grin. I smiled, accepting the picture for what it was—a brother who was worried sick and his awkward first date. "Thanks. It was just too good to pass up, and I know Easton will have wanted to see this, so . . ." I held up my phone and gave it a shake.

Tanner left to take Charlie home, and I imagined he'd take a little extra time to eat and wash the makeup off his face before returning. I sat quietly in the waiting room. The mother and son were nowhere to be found. The lone woman was grasping her phone under her chin. And the older woman was starting to doze off on the shoulder of her husband. It wasn't long before newcomers came. And slowly, one by one, someone would get called back. I was especially happy to see the woman riddled with anxiety receive good news.

I spent my time thinking about how I needed to tell Easton about the laws of a Tethered Soul. How we weren't sentenced to roam this earth forever. I needed to tell him how my time had come and how a mortal life had found me—or at least that I believed it had. I never wanted to tell him for fear it would change the course of his destiny, but as I sat in the waiting room and he lay in surgery with the idea that he was some sort of immortal hero, I knew this information was no longer a best-kept secret. He needed to be more careful.

I looked around the stagnant waiting room and racked my brain. I needed something to do. I made my way to the receptionist and asked where I could find a cup of coffee. She pointed me in the direction of the hospital cafeteria. I was walking through the halls when I ran into Dr. Faye. "John!" I said, somewhat in shock.

He gave me the same perplexed look that I had given him. "Becca? What are you doing here?" he asked, looking over my shoulder.

"Looking for coffee," I said, pointing down the hall. He nodded, confirming I was headed in the right direction.

"Yeah, down there. But what are you doing here? Is everyone OK?"

"Oh, that! Yes, um, Easton was shot. He had a kidney removed. The doctor said that he could live normally off one kidney, but that didn't sound right?" I asked, unsure if it was true.

"Oh, shit! I'm sorry to hear that! I'm heading into a c-section right now, but when I get out, I'll check up on him. Are you going to be around?" he asked.

"Yeah, I'll be here. Lindsay has Clara, so I'll be here all night. Come and find us."

"OK. Take care, I'll see you soon."

"John?" I asked.

"Yes?"

"Just one kidney?"

"Oh, yeah. He'll be fine!" John said, before disappearing behind the elevator doors. I took in a deep breath, thankful that Easton would be OK. Thankful that Clara was in good hands. That there was a doctor here I knew and trusted. And soon . . . soon, I'd be thankful for a warm cup of coffee while I waited for Easton to wake up.

CHAPTER 10

It was late when the nurse called me back. Much later than I was expecting. Even so, Tanner hadn't come back yet. I followed the nurse through a maze of hospital twists and turns—none of which I'd remember. When we came upon a single row of rooms, she gave me his room number and left me to it. Slowly, I opened his door, unsure of what I might find.

Easton lay motionless in the hospital bed, tubes under his nose and running into the crook of his arm. He looked good—better than I was expecting—like he was sleeping. His chest rose and fell under the gown, which was split slightly open. He was tucked underneath a thin sheet of the hospital bed. Not long after, a doctor came in. He checked on a few things while he updated me. The surgery went as well as expected, and he would be home soon, but he'd need to take it easy during his recovery. I took a seat next to his bed, and put Easton's warm hand in mine.

My thumb ran back and forth over his rough knuckles

as I surveyed the minor scrapes and scuffs on his forearm. I tried to imagine what had happened—the shooter, the words exchanged, the trigger pulled. How he landed and how the scrapes came to be. At first, it was simple curiosity, but quickly became a disturbing intrusion of imagery that I could no longer shut off. The fear behind his eyes would plague my dreams for years to come—even being purely speculative.

It took a while for Easton to wake. I sat patiently by his side, imagining the best way to tell him I had no more lives left—and that maybe, just maybe, he didn't either. I didn't want him to put his life in danger, but how was I to know? That could have been the thing that made his life full. It could be his key to untying his tether. And as far as I knew, it was what he wanted. He wanted the freedom to move on from this life. Could putting his life on the line to help other people be his life's fulfillment? Either way, I was afraid to tell him. So much had changed since we last talked about it. We had a family now. And who knows, maybe he'd had a change of heart?

A knock on the door startled me from my deep, troubled thoughts. I pulled my eyes off Easton and found John standing at the door. "John! Hey, how was your c-section?" I asked.

"Great! Eight pounds, six ounces. Healthy baby boy. The mom wants to name him Wilber, but the dad won't have it. How's Easton doing?" he asked, taking several steps closer to read the monitors.

I shrugged. "They said he would be awake any time, but I don't know. He's been sleeping for a while, and it doesn't look like that's going to change soon," I said, resting my gaze back on his face.

"Everyone reacts differently to the anesthesia and the procedure. He's been through a lot and just needs time to rest. It's not indicative that something is wrong. Who's his doctor?" John asked.

"Um, Dr. Sonders? Or Sanders?" I said.

"Oh, Dr. Sanders. He's a great doctor. I'll talk to him— let him know you're a friend. And if you have any questions, don't hesitate to ask. He's really personable," John said, tapping the door. It was late, and he was probably ready to go home and get some sleep between deliveries.

"I won't. Thank you," I said.

Brooklyn walked by just as John was leaving. Her eyes were puffy and face bare. "Brooklyn?" I called out as she passed by the window.

"Bec?" She popped her head in, and her face lit up as soon as she saw me. For the first time, I let go of Easton's hand, and I ran straight into Brooklyn's arms. "He's going to be OK. It's all going to be OK," she repeated.

"How did you know?" I asked. "Did Tanner call you?"

"Did I what?" Tanner asked, walking in behind her.

Brooklyn stiffened, drawing her hair behind her ear. She gave me a quick shake of the head, her eyes wide with alarm. I'd known by now what that look had meant. She must have had a dream.

"Tanner! You're back!" I said.

"Sorry it took me so long," he said, an apologetic look on his face and the remnants of pink lipstick etched into his cheeks. His eyes flickered to Brooklyn's for a quick and awkward moment, and though it was short-lived, I saw the conflict that lived in his heart. I knew he still loved Brooklyn.

"That's alright. He hasn't woken up yet," I said.

"Um, I'm not supposed to be here. They said no visitors, so I just snuck in. I've been wandering the halls for the past ten minutes hoping to find you. I'm glad I did. You haven't been answering your phone—"

"Yeah," Tanner agreed.

"Oh? It must be dead?" I picked up my phone and tried to turn it on. The screen remained black.

"But now that I've got a hold of you, and I can see you're in good company, I should go," Brooklyn said.

"No. Stay!" I replied.

Brooklyn opened her mouth, but as soon as she did, Tanner said it too. "You should stay." A soft-spoken statement that meant way more than the words themselves. Brooklyn smiled, looking down to the floor, and I brought my gaze back to Easton.

His lids twitched. Then, his brows knotted. "Hey, he's waking up!" Brooklyn said.

I squeezed his hand. "Easton? Can you hear me?" I asked. His eyes fluttered open, and his limbs woke, bending and twisting. A moan growled deep from within his throat. "Easton?" I squeezed his hand. His eyes landed on me, though they remained unfocused. He cleared his throat and tried to talk, but nothing came out except for breathy noises. "Can we get some water?" I asked, looking around the room.

"Here! There's some on this side!" Brooklyn handed me the water. Tanner stood at the foot, arms crossed and emotion clouding his face. I held the straw up to Easton's lips and he drew in a small sip. I watched as his eyes took in his brother and Brooklyn. "How are you feeling?" she asked.

"Hey, brother. You scared us," Tanner said.

A small smile spread across Easton's dry lips. "No. You don't need to be scared," he said in a raspy, hushed tone. I wiped away the single tear that dropped from my eye and smiled as relief washed over me. I kissed his knuckles repeatedly. "Where's Clara?" he asked, searching behind me.

"Lindsay has her. She's fine," I said.

"So, what happened? And why the hell didn't you have your vest on?" Tanner scolded.

Easton tried to sit up but only made it a couple of inches. I tried to help by bunching the pillows underneath his head, and Brooklyn pushed buttons on the side of the bed's arm rails. Once situated, Easton told us what happened in so many words. "I was off duty. I was coming home for dinner when I remembered I was supposed to get those drinks Charlie likes." Tanner and Brooklyn's eyes met like magnets before quickly polarizing. Her face was washed in heartbreak, his in guilt.

"I was in the back of the gas station pulling out the drinks from the refrigerator when a guy pulled out his gun. He tried robbing the clerk, but he was a stubborn son of a bitch. He wouldn't give him the money."

"Oh shit," Tanner mumbled into his cupped hand.

"Yeah. He turned his gun on a mom and her son. As soon as he did, the clerk pulled out his own gun. I made my way to the boy and his mom. I took the perp down, but not before he got a shot off." Easton rubbed his hand over the bandage.

"Oh, man. You should have just stayed in uniform until you got home!" Tanner said.

"I was off duty!"

"Still!"

"But I had dinner," Easton said. "Honestly, it was a freak accident. I was lucky to be there when I was."

"Lucky?" I hissed.

"Yeah. I was able to save that boy and his mom. Who knows what would have happened if I wasn't there," Easton said, his voice full once again.

"But who knows what would have happened if you were shot a little higher?" I scowled.

"I do," Easton said, challenging me. But the truth was, he didn't know. None of us did. Except for maybe Brooklyn. But if she did, she wasn't talking about it. I shook my head, barely able to control myself in front of Tanner. I looked away, mauling the inside of my cheek.

"I saved not one life but two! I did it!" Easton said, looking up at his brother.

"You did it . . ." Tanner said, a proud smile across his face.

"I can't wait to do it again!" Easton coughed and grabbed at his side, wincing. Tanner came to his side, and their hands met before he enveloped him in a hug.

"You did it," Tanner repeated. I don't know what goals

they had set when becoming police officers, but I was teetering on the edge of concern and alarm.

"I'm glad you're OK, but don't do that again!" Brooklyn said.

"Thank you!" I said in response to her statement.

"What? No! That's my job!" Easton frowned. Both boys turned against Brooklyn and me.

"Your job is to get shot, off duty?" she asked.

"Hey, that's not fair." Tanner came to Easton's defense.

"Well, maybe if he had worn his vest until he got home . . ." she said.

"Well, maybe if he vowed to protect the innocent, then he should do that at all costs and not just when he's on the clock," Tanner dug in. At this point, it was clear they weren't arguing about Easton's safety anymore.

"OK. OK. Can we just celebrate that the boy and his mom are OK? That I'm OK?" Easton asked. And as worried as I was that he may have laid down his life under false impressions, I could agree to celebrate his safety—along with that of the mother and child.

"Yes," I said. "We're so happy you're OK."

"Wait, what about the clerk?" Brooklyn asked. And when Easton gave a slow shake of his head, the room fell silent. ". . . And the shooter?" she asked a moment later.

"I don't think he's going to make it either. They weren't loading him into the ambulance when I was taken away." The room grew quiet once more.

"Hey, looks like you're awake . . ." A nurse walked in, surveying the room. "And there's a party in here. Visiting hours are over. Didn't anyone tell you that?" she asked, one hand on her hip.

"Oh, yeah. I was just leaving," Brooklyn said.

"Me too." Tanner placed his hand on the small of Brooklyn's back and ushered her out. She turned, blowing us a kiss goodbye. And I watched them walk away together. His hand was still resting on her back as they disappeared down the hallway.

"And you, Miss?" the nurse asked me.

"Me? I'm his wife," I said.

"I'm sorry. But no visitors overnight. You can come back in the morning," she said.

"But—"

"It's OK, Beck. Nurse . . ." Easton squinted at the nurse's name tag. "Nurse Shannon is going to take good care of me. Isn't that right?" he asked.

"That's right, Mr. Green. Now say your goodbyes. I'll give you a minute, but then I'm coming back for your checkup," she said. I watched the nurse until her back disappeared from view before turning to Easton.

"I don't want to leave you," I said.

"It's OK. I'll be alright. It's just one night."

I frowned. He didn't know that any more than I did. I stood, bending over the bed, and kissed his forehead. "I love you," I said.

"I love you, too. Honestly, I'm OK. And remember, even if I wasn't, we have a backup plan. May 7 we meet at the bridge. Never forget," Easton said. And for the first time since he woke, I could see the seriousness of the situation touch down upon him. Our plan had always been that if we were to separate, we'd meet again on the bridge. On our anniversary.

"Honey," I said, half-joking, half-serious. "Don't make me change your diapers."

"What?" Easton said. Shocked, he grabbed at his side.

"If you didn't make it . . . I wasn't going to wait until you were old enough to meet me at the bridge. I was going to find you. Now. I was going to call every hospital in the world to find you. And when I did, I would have adopted you." Easton smiled at me with admiration. "But, you know what?" I asked.

"What?"

"You wouldn't be my husband anymore . . . You'd be my son. And that shit's weird. So don't do it!" I jabbed my pointer into his chest. I was serious, but he was laughing, even through the pain. "I'm serious, Easton!" I said as the nurse came in, tapping her watch.

"OK. I won't. I won't do that to you. I promise," Easton said, holding up his hands.

I gave him my most serious glare before turning my back on him. The nurse chuckled when she saw Easton's face wrapped in both pain and pleasure. And as I walked out of the room I heard her say, "Oh, you're in trouble, aren't you?" I nodded silently because he was.

CHAPTER 11

The next couple of days, Easton spent recovering in the hospital, and I juggled my new position as Nora's nanny. It was in Easton's absence that Nora's company was even more than a joy, it was a welcomed distraction. Having her in my car, at my dinner table, and under my roof was more than welcomed. It filled a hole in my heart that I once thought would never heal. And I caught myself frequently with my hand over my heart and tears in my eyes.

Nora was a Tethered Soul. She had already proved that to be true. But occasionally, I thought that Clara wasn't. And that idea had come more often since I had been acting as Nora's nanny. I watched her carefully, and she'd become distracted frequently. The "lights," she'd call them. She tried to hide it as much as possible in my presence, and it made me sad to think she was uncomfortable around me.

However, when she didn't think that I was watching or

listening, she spoke of them freely, like an imaginary friend. Clara loved it and asked questions every time it came up. I wondered what Lindsay thought of it all, but that only reminded me I had to have a very serious conversation with her one day about Nora, and I didn't want to think about that.

It was only a couple of days that Easton spent recovering in the hospital, but I quickly became used to my new routine. I took the girls to school in the morning, visited Easton in the hospital, picked up the girls, took Nora to dance, went back to the hospital, and then home for dinner. Nora was picked up each night at varying times, and it was the night that Easton was discharged from the hospital that Nora was staying over for the first time. Lindsay had the night shift, and John was on call for delivery. It was the first night that my family would sleep under one roof, and I couldn't be more grateful for Lindsay's schedule. Nora seemed happy, too.

Easton tried to eat dinner at the dining table, but he was too uncomfortable. The girls had no problem joining Easton on the sofa with their dinner plates. And I could barely eat I was so excited. I had my husband home, safe. And I had both of my girls giggling before me. But as I had learned before, it was in happy moments that sometimes I'd feel the sorrow creep in. I knew it wouldn't always be like this, and that one day, Nora would sit in the living room with a different family, feeling lost and lonely. We'd all be nothing but memories for her to fall back on. When I couldn't shake the thought of it, I cleared plates and cleaned up in the kitchen.

"It's time to turn the lights off. You have school tomorrow, and we need to wake up ready to learn. Did you girls brush your teeth?" I asked. Both girls tucked under the same blanket. One towheaded, one with dark wild hair, and both with pale dimpled cheeks.

"Yes," they said, giggling.

I turned out the lights and stumbled over the bedside. I hugged Clara and whispered, "I love you."

"I love you," she said.

Then I reached over Clara and wrapped my arms around Nora. "I love you," I said.

Nora jolted back, and I worried that I'd upset her. "What's that?" she asked.

"What's what?" I looked around in the dark, and my eyes were adjusted enough to see Nora holding her arms out wide and looking between the two.

"Oh. It's nothing." She reached for me again, and I wrapped my arms around her for a second try. This time, she jumped back. "What is that?!" she gasped.

"I felt it too," I said.

"It tingles?" she asked.

"It's like electricity," I laughed. Nora nodded in agreement and laughed, too.

"I want to feel!" Clara grabbed me and knew I had to act quickly. I dug my fingers into her ribs and tickled her.

"Buzzz!" I said, tickling both girls. They squealed and jumped, giggled and squirmed. I laughed until the room glowed with twinkling stars as bright as the northern sky. And though Nora said nothing, she too had fallen quiet with searching eyes. It wasn't fair that Clara couldn't see the love, but what was most important was that she could feel it. And that she had. I kissed her forehead, and she smiled up at me, unaware of the twinkling night sky within her four bedroom walls, and we said goodnight.

I lay down on Easton's lap in the living room, and he ran his hands through my hair. I didn't say anything for a long while. Not that I didn't know what to say . . . but that I didn't know how to start.

"Hey, Easton?" I asked.

"Huh?"

"I think Nora is Tethered." It pained me to say it.

"Oh, yeah. For sure," he said.

A moment passed before I continued. "But I don't think Clara is . . ."

Easton sighed, and it took him some time before his eyes met mine. "I think you may be right. We're just going to have to give her the best life we can. Encourage her to live it right the first time," he said.

"Well, I mean . . . we need to teach them both that, right?"

"Yeah. But you know what I mean. Nora will have more time to learn it all."

"But what if we're not here to teach her?" I asked.

Easton frowned. "What do you mean? We'll always be here for her." Easton had been thinking it was Clara that he had limited time with, while I was worried about Nora living eternity, alone.

It was then that I found myself with the opportunity to tell him what I had been holding back for so long. "I think this is my last chance, Easton. I don't think I'll be moving on to a third life," I said.

"What are you talking about? Of course, you will. That's how it works," he said, concern still at bay.

"But what if you don't know how it works?" Easton's fingers froze in my hair, and his palm rested heavily on my head. "Brooklyn has been around for much longer than you, and she says there's a way out."

"A way out?" he said, craning to look at me clearly. I sat up when his leg shifted under my head.

"Yeah. Do you want that?" I asked. Easton's jaw dropped open and hung as his eyes searched mine for answers. "I mean, I know you *did*. But do you *still*?"

"Well, a lot has changed, Beck. Why are you just telling me this now? How long have you known there might be another option for us?" he asked.

"Um, for a while," I admitted.

"How long, Beck?"

I looked away. "Since before we married," I said, softly.

"What?!" his voice raised.

"Shhh, the girls are trying to sleep," I said.

Easton twisted and groaned, grabbing at his side as he tried to stand. I reached my hand out to help, but he didn't accept it.

"Let me explain . . ." I pled.

"I just . . . can you just give me a moment? I need to wrap my head around this before we go any further," he said, heading for the door.

"Wait!" I called out, but the door closed behind him. I

stood in the middle of the living room, my thoughts on Easton alone. I didn't want him to be mad at me, and I probably should have told him sooner. I *definitely* should have told him sooner. It took everything I had to sit back down and give him the space he needed, but I did so staring at the door knob, willing him to come back. When I heard his car door shut and the window lit from his headlights, I promised myself that I'd never keep a secret from him again. No matter how big, how small, or how hurtful. I'd never do it again.

Easton came home that night before I fell asleep. When he walked in and saw me sitting right where he left me, his face softened. He strode toward me and took a seat by my side, grimacing as he leaned back. Once comfortable, he nodded. "OK. I'm ready. Explain," he said.

I took a deep breath and began. "Brooklyn says that we're tethered because we had an unfair disadvantage. We were taken before our time for one reason or another. Most likely for the greater good. That being a Tethered Soul is like getting alternative compensation—only, some of us don't want it. She says that it was never meant to be forever. And that more often than not, a Tethered Soul will only take one extra life." I spoke clearly and slowly, allowing him the time he needed to take it all in. But he didn't need more time than he had already taken on his drive. He urged me to continue.

"She said that our tether would last as long as needed to get one *full* life in. Once we achieved our best life, then we would be rightfully compensated, and we would move on. Just like everyone else."

"A full life? What does that even mean?" he asked.

I pulled my leg up on the sofa, gripping my shin. I couldn't tell how he was taking the news, and I worried more with every bit of new information I gave him. "Brooklyn said that sometimes, being tethered can backfire. And that's when a Tethered Soul becomes stranded and ultimately turns to a Tortured Soul." I watched him carefully. "She says that's what you are . . ."

"What about her? She's been here longer than I have. Why hasn't she lived her one life then?" Easton asked, skeptical.

"Because she doesn't want to die. She likes it here." I shrugged.

"Then how is she continuing to live? How does she make sure she doesn't have a full—" Easton paused, his eyes trailing off into the distance. "She won't marry Tanner," he said softly. I nodded. "She doesn't want kids . . ." he said, cupping his mouth. His eyes met mine in question. "You knew this *before* we married? *Before* we had our girls?"

"I did," I admitted.

Easton ran his hands through his hair. I knew what he was thinking. He was thinking that I chose a life with him that would end, when I could have chosen one that lasted forever.

But that's not what I saw. I saw the quality of our lives meaning more than the minutes, the days, and the years we'd spend here. "I didn't want to tell you. I thought I'd be messing with fate. I wanted you to live your best life, but I only wanted it for you when you were ready to take it. I didn't want to be the reason you forced it. I didn't want you to go . . . *uncompensated*," I said with a shrug. I didn't know how else to say it.

"Do you think that I've lived tortured all these lives because I wouldn't allow myself to love?" he asked. It hurt to hear. To think that he had been walking this earth for centuries trying to protect his heart, but all he was doing was hurting himself in the long run.

"It's not for me to say. Maybe?"

"And now, that we have each other . . . now that we have our daughters, you think we're living our last lives? That our time is limited?" he asked.

"I believe mine is." I couldn't explain it. It was just a feeling I had.

"And mine?"

"I don't know, Easton. I don't know what a full life looks like for you. All I know is that I feel it in my heart. I feel it when I look at you, and I feel it when the girls giggle. I feel it when I laugh with Brooklyn, and when Lindsay hugs me. I just know that I was lucky to have another chance at life. And I know that I took it."

Easton's eyes locked onto mine as he absorbed what I had said. "I never took it. I was too broken to even try." Easton hung his head and mindlessly rubbed his side where his kidney had once been.

"You have to be careful at work, Easton. You might not be coming back again," I said. He looked at me, his eyes wide with the realization that things weren't what they seemed. "You might not be as invincible as you once thought."

The corners of his lips curved ever so slightly. "I can graduate," he said.

"What do you mean?"

"All my lives, it was like never graduating. Never moving on to the next level. No progression, no advancement. But now, I can earn it. And I want to. I've wanted to earn it since the day I met you. My lives were stagnant before I met you. But they've been in motion ever since. You opened up my heart and not just to you but to everyone. My brother, my adopted parents . . . You gave me Clara and Nora . . . You gave me my full life. If Brooklyn was right, and that's all it took to graduate, then I was already on my way."

Easton took my hand in his and kissed my knuckles. "I don't want you to ever think that you need to hide something from me. We're in this together. Right?" he asked.

"Right. You're so right! I'm so sorry, I don't know what I was thinking. I'll never hide anything from you again. I'm done with secrets!"

"Promise?" he asked.

"Promise."

"Then you need to tell Lindsay about Nora," he said.

It hit like a ton of bricks dropping into my lap. "I know I do. Soon." I nodded.

"Soon." Easton pulled me into his arms and called out when I leaned against his wound.

"Oh! I'm so sorry!" I said. He shook his head and pulled me into him again. I hugged him more carefully this time. I lay on him, feeling light as air. Feeling closer to him than I ever had before. The heat from his chest warmed my cheek, and I took in one long, cleansing breath. A breath that was pure and hopeful. Until . . .

"Poor Nora . . ." he said.

CHAPTER 12

I found myself in the parking lot of Sunny Hill Assisted Living, unable to bring myself in. I knew I'd face my mother, and she'd face a stranger. I'd be no different to her than any other person she would see today. Another face in a sea of people she could no longer recognize. The relentless fear in her eyes was heartbreaking, and I knew that today would be no different. I felt the guilt flow through my veins as I sat in my truck. How dare I not be eager to see her . . . to try and improve her day. But I *wasn't* eager. I didn't want to look into the eyes of my flesh and blood—the eyes of the woman who raised me . . . and know she saw nothing in return. I didn't want to do it.

It would be different if I had Tommy. Or even Bodie. Because if I walked through those doors with a leash in my hand, I'd know that I could bring a smile to my mom's face. She wouldn't recognize me, of course, but she would be smiling. Her fear would be pushed to the outskirts of her mind, and for a moment . . . just a moment . . . she'd be happy. As happy as she could be these days. I wanted that for her. I wanted to be the one to bring that to her. And selfishly, I wanted to walk through those doors and know that my heart wouldn't be ripped from my chest.

I sighed. Taking my bag in my hand, I locked my truck and started for the doors. Lindsay wasn't working today, so I'd be on my own. I could do it. At least that's what I told myself.

"Good morning. Are you visiting today?"

"Yes. Beck in room 306."

"Oh, lovely. She could use a smile today. Just sign in here." I looked at the woman behind the desk, trying to decipher what she meant when she said that my mother could use a smile today. It didn't sound like a good thing, and I was sure I needed to prepare for an uphill battle. My stomach twisted, tying in knots.

"Thank you," I said, setting the pen down. I stalled before the door, my eyes fixed on the 306 tacked to the wall. I knew some days were better than others; Lindsay had warned me of that. And I had only seen my mother a couple of times since she had been in the home. Each time had been like the time before. She was quiet. Timid. Distant. I didn't have it in me to see her on a bad day, but I couldn't give up on her. What kind of daughter would I be then? I twisted the knob and slowly opened the door, peeking my head in.

"Hello?" I said. Mom sat in bed, gazing out the window. "Good morning, Mrs. Beck. How are you today?" I asked, knowing I wouldn't get an answer. She didn't acknowledge me.

I placed my bag down on the table and sat at the edge of her bed. When I took her hand in mine, she slowly turned to look at me. I smiled warmly at her, and for a second, I thought she felt something. But then, like every other time, she turned away, indifferent. I wanted to shake her—tell her she had to remember me. Tell her I missed her and that I was sorry for leaving her the way that I did. That I was sorry for ruining her life.

"Look," she said, pointing out the window.

Look? She's talking?

I looked out the window, arching my back to see what she had been pointing at. I craned my neck, looking all around, but saw nothing. "What is it?" I asked.

"Look . . . an angel . . ."

Cold chills ran down my spine. I saw no angel beyond the window pane, and I had seen no such thing when I died, but that didn't mean she didn't see it now. I looked out the window again, but still, there was nothing but the lush green garden of unpickable roses. I turned back to her, the morning sun lighting up her eyes. "It's beautiful," I said.

I wiped my clammy hands off on my jeans and pulled my hair back into a ponytail. Her gaze remained on the angel. "Breakfast time, Mrs. Beck." A young nurse backed into the room, holding a tray of food. "Oh! I didn't realize she had company!"

"Hello," I said, helping her guide the tray to a nearby table. "I'm B . . . Becca."

"I'm Christine. Nice to meet you. She hasn't been eating

very well lately. Would you mind trying to get her to take a few bites while you're here?" Christine asked.

"Oh, sure. I don't mind."

"Thank you. I'll be by later to get the tray," she said.

"Thanks, Christine." She gave me a polite smile and moved on to deliver more breakfast that would go uneaten and unacknowledged. *It must feel like a thankless job*, I thought. The eggs looked wet and the toast brittle. "Are you hungry, Mom?" I asked. My heart-stopping as it slipped from my mouth. But her gaze was still set on the angel outside her window, and I realized that she didn't know any better. I could call her Mom if I wanted. And I could tell her all the things that I wished I had before I died. I had a golden ticket here to say whatever I wanted . . . Whatever, I *needed*. And why shouldn't I?

"Mom?" I whispered, looking for subtle hints of recollection in her eyes. "Mom, do you remember me?"

Not so much as a blink of her eyes. I was relieved at first, but on the edge of that relief was regret for not getting to her sooner. *I should have* . . . I squeezed her hand and took down the facade, piece by piece.

"I should have . . . come back for Easton's shoe." I dropped my gaze to our hands. Both similar—one kissed by the wrinkles of time and the other gifted with renewal. Our fingers were the same shape . . . or had been before her knuckles grew with arthritis. It was likely the reason that she didn't wear her wedding band.

"I should have knocked on your door. Journals in hand. We could have gone through them together. I know you would have been sad. Maybe even a little angry, and that would have been OK, too. But I should have come back for you. And I didn't. I should have done it the very second I remembered my life with you and Dad. I should have . . . I *could* have . . . haunted Carter." I chuckled.

My cheeks were tight as I pondered the many ways I could have gotten him back for all the pranks he played on me as a kid. But they slackened when my fun-loving imagination showed me the more realistic fallout. Carter wouldn't find it funny and neither would I. I sighed, dispelling the thought that any of this could ever be fun.

"I'm sorry I left you. It wasn't by choice. I never would have gotten in that car had I known I would've done that to you and Pop. I know my time was limited as it was, but I had months longer to say the things I needed to, and it was all taken away too fast. Maybe I would have come to grips with the idea of dying, and I would have opened up more. I could have accepted it, and then I could have told my friends, my aunt, my teachers, and co-workers. I could have told everyone, and I could have felt the love and support that I know everyone was robbed of giving me. I could have leaned on them. On you. And it would have given you time to prepare, too. I'm sure there are a lot of things you wanted to say to me that you never had the chance to get out. Or simply hugged me a little longer . . . but we can do that now, can't we?" I asked.

Afraid to look at her, I refused to raise my eyes. My body felt heavy like someone had draped a weighted blanket over my shoulders, and I succumbed to the pressure. Folding in on myself, I let go of my mom's hand and laid my head down on her lap. Her tiny lap. I curled myself onto the edge of her bed as she lay still. It didn't feel like it had when I was a kid seeking the comfort of my mother. She was no longer the stronger of us, and I was no longer afraid. I didn't lay across her lap because I was scared, but more because I needed her love, and she wouldn't give it to me. She *couldn't* give it to me. So, I rest my head on her thin, brittle legs, and I pretended that she pulled me into her embrace like the last hug I never got.

When I felt her hand drop to the edge of the bed, my eyes dampened, wishing that it had fallen to my shoulder or that she had played with my hair the way she once had. "You're going to be OK, Mom. I know you've had a hard life. No parent should ever have to bury their child. Even I can't understand what you went through, and once upon a time, I lost my Molly. I know you questioned life for a long time after I died. And I know you never found an answer. But the world kept spinning, and you kept living. It's hard to live with a broken heart. I know that. I've felt that. But Pop is waiting for you. Somewhere, he's waiting for you. And you're going to be alright." The door cracked open, and I startled, jolting the bed.

"Oh, I'm sorry to interrupt. I'm collecting trays." A nurse backed into the room, wheeling a cart. I sat up and wiped the tears from my eyes.

"It's OK," I said.

The nurse looked at me for just a moment and nodded. She had seen it all before. "Family?" she asked, softly.

I had never seen this nurse before, and Mom wouldn't say any differently. "Yes," I admitted. She smiled with empathy.

"She likes the pudding the most, but even that she hasn't been eating. I see today is no different. I'll leave it behind for her, in case you can get her to take a few bits, and I'll take everything else with me."

"Thank you," I said, as the nurse excused herself.

I peeled back the lid and sank a plastic spoon into the vanilla pudding. I held out a small spoonful, but she was disinterested. "Still looking at your angel?" I asked. Her face lit up with a rosy glow, and the corners of her lips pulled upward. I chuckled to myself, and she found it to be contagious. When she started to laugh, I did too, and it snowballed from there. Before I knew it, Mom and I were laughing together, just like old times. Only this time, I didn't know what we were laughing at, and neither did she. As soon as the laughter came, it passed by like a rogue wave—there one minute, gone the next. And the wake was just a silent reminder of all the things we didn't have to share because of her dementia.

I stood by the side table, setting her pudding pack down. My attention kept finding its way back to my bag and the contents that hid within. I glanced at my mom, who was watching the garden like a feature film. "Hey, I brought something I wanted to show you," I said, making my way to the bag. I slipped my hand inside and pulled out my journals, tied once again with the burlap bow. Just like my mom had them displayed. "Do you remember these?" I asked, bringing them to her side. She looked down at them, her expression unchanged.

"I told you not to read them because there were some things in here I didn't want you to see. I always figured you'd read them, anyway. But you didn't." I untied the bow, and she watched, more intrigued than I had seen her since coming to Sunny Hill Assisted Living. I flipped to the last few pages in the journal where I had kept my goodbye letters. I took out the envelope marked "Mom" and opened it for the first time, running my finger underneath the seal. I unfolded the letter and held it in my shaky hands. Nine pages of goodbyes and regrets.

"Mom," I began. "I'm sorry I never told you about my illness. I don't want you to worry. And I can't bear to look into your eyes for my final months and see a broken woman. I just want everything to remain as normal as could be. I need it too. I need my parents to be strong and supportive because if you were anything less, then I might crumble. And I don't have the strength for that, nor the time." I paused in reflection, remembering a life where time was fleeting.

"I'm so tired, Mom, and I can feel my body deceiving me. Forgive me for keeping that burden to myself, but it's not one that I want to share. You don't have to worry about me. I'm not alone in this. I've met someone. He's kind of cute in his own way. Not really my type, but I think he found his way into my life for a reason. It's weird because I feel like I can talk to him. And I need someone I can open up to right now. Someone who can support me but who isn't already a pillar in my life. I hope you understand."

I flipped the page, appreciating the bittersweetness to the memories of a time when Easton was just an ember in my heart. A mysterious stranger. I'd hoped he would be a light for me in a time of darkness, but little did I know that he would be so much more. I read page after page of memories that I held dear to my heart—and a few apologies for things I never moved on from. My eyes burned by the time I reached the ending.

"Mom, I know you will be sad when you read this one day, and that's the last thing I want for you. So for me, if you don't mind, could you look back and remember me for all the good times? The laughs, the messes made, and lessons learned? Because the suffering pales in comparison to all the fun we had and the love we shared. And I'll be fine. I don't know what will happen to me after I'm gone, but I'll be OK. Because I'm the strong and capable woman you raised me to be. So, thank you for giving me the best parts of yourself. It was the best part of my life. I love you, always. Till we meet again, Everly . . ."

Till we meet again. I never thought it would be like this. Slowly, I folded the nine-page letter and tucked it back into its envelope. Mom's frail hand grabbed hold of my wrist, and I was taken aback to see her looking into my eyes. Not past them or through them but directly into them. Not just who I was now but the girl I'd always been. She saw me. *Me.* Tears welled in her eyes. She said nothing, but she didn't need words to express all that she had in that moment. I could *feel* it. "Mom?" I whispered, heart thumping in my chest.

"How did she do?" the nurse asked, barging in on the most fragile and, unfortunately, fleeting moment. As soon as I looked away, the bond had broken. Mom's grip was still tight around my wrist, but she was no longer looking at me or anything in particular. Not even the angel in the garden.

"Um . . ." I began. Not wanting to move on.

"You said this was Mom? I think your brother just got here!"

"What?!"

"Yeah, Mr. Beck just signed in. You have to see these flowers he brought . . ."

I pried my mom's fingers from my wrist. My heart pounding in my chest as I jumped to my feet and fled the room. The nurse whirled around as I burst through the door. I nearly ran straight into Carter, a pair of legs walking a grand bouquet of white lilies. "Oh!" I gasped, spinning on my heels as he lifted the bouquet to see who he'd nearly run into.

"Sorry! Didn't see you there!" he said. But I was already down the hall in a half-jog. And I knew that while I'd managed to grab my bag, I left behind the journals and all of my goodbye letters . . . including Carter's.

It was a perfect Sunday morning—lazy, slow. I was tangled up in bedsheets and Easton when the doorbell rang. Only, I hadn't been expecting anyone. "Who's that?" I asked Easton. He shrugged, just as confused as I was. I slipped on pajama pants and a robe and hobbled down the hall. I saw Brooklyn through the peephole, holding a tray of coffees. But when I opened the door, she was no longer the center of my attention, and neither were her caffeinated gifts.

Black shaggy hair covered the lonely eyes of Bodie as he sat on my doorstep; leash wrapped around Brooklyn's hand. "What?!" I shrieked. The dog lurched forward to smell me.

Brooklyn shrugged, a big smile on her face as she held out the leash for me to take. "He's all yours," she said. My throat swelled and my eyes burned as I kneeled down slowly. Bodie's tail wagged slowly as he sniffed my face.

"Hi, Bodie! Hi!" I said, scratching behind his ears.

"What's going on?" Easton came to the door in a pair of sweatpants and nothing else. His incision was purple and still somewhat inflamed. My eyes dropped, lingering on the shadow of his obliques. "Morning, Brooklyn. Who's this? Did you get a dog?" Easton leaned down to pet Bodie.

"He's deaf," I said.

"He's *yours*," Brooklyn laughed.

Easton stiffened, pointing in question to his bare chest. Brooklyn nodded as we waited to see how he would take the news. "Mine? Like here? In *this* house?" He pointed to the hardwood floor, frozen like a statue, but I imagined his mind was racing.

"Please!" I said, hugging Bodie around the neck.

"How old is he?" he asked. I looked to Bodie and the tips of white hair on his chin.

Brooklyn's shoulders dropped as she thrust the tray of coffee toward Easton's chest. "Seven or eight," she said, letting herself in.

"Come on. Come on, Bodie," I encouraged. But he didn't need to be babied; he was all smiles and tail wags.

"Well, is a deaf dog going to be safe with Clara?" Easton asked. I stilled, looking to Brooklyn for answers. He hung in the doorway, unconvinced.

"He's perfect for her. I had a dream about it. They're already best buds!" she said.

"Yeah!" I agreed, fully trusting Brooklyn's gifts. Easton sighed, knowing he had lost the battle before it even started. He set the coffees down on the kitchen counter, and I took the leash off Bodie.

"Thanks for the coffee," Easton said, taking a sip and

making himself comfortable on the sofa.

"Yeah, thanks for the coffee . . . and the *dog!* How did you even get him? They never returned any of my calls. Oh, my god . . . Did you steal him?" My mind spun a web of lies —all of the things I would say if we ever got caught.

"What? No!" she said.

"Of course not," I shook my head, thankful.

"I've been working with Sandy behind the scenes. I asked her to keep it a secret from you, and she was more than willing." I looked up at Brooklyn, remembering the conversation we had in the car. She was worried that I didn't need her now that I had my first best friend back in the picture. I jumped to my feet to give her a hug. Bodie flinched, and I froze midway to her. Then, ever so slowly, I wrapped my arms around her. "You don't need to do that," she said.

"Thank you, Brooklyn. He's the best gift anyone's ever given me . . ."

"Hey!" Easton grumbled from the living room.

"Did you hear that, Easton?" Brooklyn laughed. "Well, you're welcome. You deserve him. And I think he'll make you happy."

"Yeah, and my mom, too!" I said. I'd been so excited, scratching the back of Bodie's ear that I barely caught the troubled look in Brooklyn's eyes as she turned away.

"So, you said you had a dream that Bodie would be good for Clara?" Easton asked.

"Uh-huh," Brooklyn sipped her coffee.

"Do you remember, back at campus, when you told me you had a dream of Beck and me dying?" Easton asked, and the air shifted in the room, turning the buzzing energy into a frigid chill. Where was he going with this?

"Yeah, I remember."

"Well, I always thought that you dreamed about the car accident. I thought it was weird that you had a dream like that, but we had already died, so I just thought nothing of it—"

"Shhh, keep your voice down," I said, my neck craning towards Clara's room. Her door was still closed.

"—but now, I'm worried that what you saw wasn't a vision of the past."

Brooklyn sat across from Easton, and I remained on the floor with the dog, watching, waiting.

"No. It wasn't of the car accident, though I saw that, too," Brooklyn said, pausing for a long moment.

"Can you tell us what you saw then? Because you show up with this dog and these dreams, and I know there's always more to the story than you willingly tell."

Brooklyn's eyes flickered to mine, and my stomach dropped. Did I want to know? She'd never shared this with me before, and I assumed it was for good reason. But then again, I'd never asked. It could have been as simple as that.

Before I knew it, both of them were looking at me in question, and I knew it was up to me to decide if I wanted to hear about how I would die. Just because I had done it once before, didn't make it any easier. It was still just scary and unnerving. "OK. It's OK," I said, seeking comfort in the eyes of Bodie.

"Are you sure you want to know?" Brooklyn asked.

"I mean . . . I don't know? You tell me," I said, dumping

the decision on her.

She nodded, then began. "It's a terrible storm. Worst one in a decade—"

"Wait!" I said. "Are you sure?"

Brooklyn stared at me, considering my doubt, but ultimately began again. "You're older—seventy maybe. Your hair is white." Brooklyn motioned to her head as her eyes lost their focus. Chills crawled down my spine, and I pulled Bodie close.

"You're wearing a teal scarf and these tiger's eye drop earrings that you cherish. I don't know why. Your lips are red like you know it's your last day and you want to dress up one last time," she said, brows knitted. I could see the hurt in her eyes as she walked through her vision.

A moment passed—long enough for Easton and me to worry. Our eyes met the moment she began again. "It's peaceful. You're in bed, nearly sleeping when it happens. There are flowers. They're beautiful . . ." Brooklyn trails off, her eyes squinting as she tries to pull herself back to the present moment. I rubbed the goosebumps from my arms and failed to meet the eyes of my husband.

"And she doesn't come back?" Easton asked, softly. "Her tether . . . It's broken?"

I looked up to Brooklyn and found that her face was twisted in grief and something else—maybe regret or uncertainty. I couldn't tell. "I . . . I'm not certain she ever *was* tethered," she said.

"What?" Easton asked.

I opened my mouth, but the words never came. The room was silent for what felt like an eternity. "I'm not sure!

I don't know! I mean, yes, she was tethered . . ." She stumbled over her words. I let out a breath of air and glanced at Easton, worried. ". . . but, maybe not in the way that you always thought her to be."

"What are you talking about, Brooklyn? If there's anything you know, you need to say it now. Just say it," Easton demanded.

"You see, Easton and I are tethered to this earth, right? But, I *think*—I don't *know*—that Becca is tethered to *you* . . ."

"To me?" Easton asked.

"Yes, you." Easton and I looked at one another, and I felt gravity itself shift beneath me. "Easton, you couldn't get your life to make sense. All your chances and you never seemed to get it right. But there was an answer to all your questions. It was as simple as love. But not just any love. It had to be a love so strong and so deep that it would flip your world upside down. Becca was the only one that could do that for you. And in the process, I think her soul got wrapped around yours. The circumstances weren't quite right with her cancer and all. Your heart needed more time —more experience. The only remedy was a second chance at first love."

"So, I never had more lives?" I asked Brooklyn.

"No. At least, I don't think so . . . While your life wasn't perfect by any means, it was still enough. A Tethered Soul is usually seen when a child is taken too soon. You were far from being a child when you received your diagnosis. And that's why I can't help but wonder if you were ever tethered at all."

"Then, why all the talk about living forever? About

mediocracy being the key to eternity? Why would you lie about that?" I demanded, anger boiling under my skin, making the nape of my neck heat.

"Well, like I said, I don't know for certain. And it's confusing. I'm only human. I make mistakes, too!" she said defensively.

"How do you know any of this? Any of it at all?" Easton pried.

Brooklyn sighed, throwing her head back onto the sofa. "OK. I'm . . . a caseworker, if you will. It doesn't really have an official name, but that's beside the point. The point is that my gift, coupled with my Tethered Soul, makes me a unique piece in this game."

"Game?" I asked.

"Well, no. It's not a game, but for the sake of analogy . . . if it were a game of chess, and everyone was pawns taking one step forward at a time, your Tethered Souls would be the horses. You move in unique ways compared to all the other players. Different rules apply to you. But then there's me, and I'd be the queen because I can move almost any way I want to."

"Who's the king?" Easton asked.

"What?"

"The king. If we're playing chess, who's the king?" he said.

"No. We're not playing chess. All I'm saying is that it's my job to protect you. It's my job to help you get to the other side of the board. And I do that with my gift. My knowledge of the past and future. It's like the queen's ability to move in many directions around the board."

"So, no king," Easton confirmed.

"I was there the day you two met. On the bridge. Did you know that?" Brooklyn stood and paced the length of the room.

"I had been following Easton's case after having a dream about him. I found him nearly a month later after having a dream every single night about his empty heart. His need for a soul unlike any other. The perfect companion suited for his special situation."

"You were there?" I asked in awe.

"Situation?" Easton asked.

"Yeah. You had lived so long, everyone bored you. Everyone was predictable," she said, and Easton nodded in agreement. "You had to fall for a heart that needed you as desperately as you needed it. And that was none other than the dying heart of Everly Beck," she said.

My insides twisted with a weird sensation; like butterflies in the stomach, but much higher, swirling in my chest and escaping into my throat where the cancer had once been.

"I started having dreams of the both of you at dinner with a note—a contract of sorts. A stolen kiss in the parking lot. And dancing in a field, till the rain fell. I knew it was my job to help secure the path for you. And when Easton was having trouble with his car on the day you two met and he walked to the bridge in that awful storm, I knew the entire plan would be thrown out the window."

I glanced at Easton as his eyes fixed on recollection. I never knew he had car troubles that day, but I had always wondered how he got to the bridge without a car in sight. It gave merit to Brooklyn's story, though I didn't need it. I already believed her.

"I went to Beck's doctor's appointment, pretending to be the patient before her. I ate up twice as much time as the doctor allowed. When your appointment was pushed back an hour, you hadn't even noticed," she said.

"You saw me?" I asked, and Bodie nudged my hand gently.

"Yeah, I saw you in the waiting room. You were so lost. You needed Easton just as badly as he needed you after roaming this earth for three hundred years . . . I watched you two at the coffee shop, and I was there at that wedding you crashed. I crashed it too," she said with a laugh. The memories came back to me like shattered pieces of glass— there but distorted. Had I seen Brooklyn at the wedding?

"When you two died, I had another case I needed to work on. I wrapped it up as quickly as possible. It was a year's time before I could follow you."

"You followed us?"

"I had to. I'd never loved a case as much as I did yours. I knew Easton would spend his life trying to find you, so I set out looking for you first, Becca. I got parents near your home, and I made sure we became friends. I was always there for you, even when you didn't know it," she said.

"But how? How did you pick your parents?" I asked.

"Remember, I move differently. I have more options because I've dedicated myself to helping people just like you. People who are lost . . . the tethered and tortured," Brooklyn said, the pacing finally slowing to a point where she could sit back down. It helped put me at ease, but nothing worked quite like Bodie when he rested his head on my lap.

"The case of Easton's heart captured mine in a way no other case had. But nothing was better than being your friend, Becca. At first, it was just part of the job, but quickly, I opened my heart to you in the same way Easton had. And I hadn't done that in a very, very long time. It was so nice having a friend—a genuine friend—that sometimes . . . I lost my way. Sometimes, I didn't want the job anymore. And sometimes, I'd have given it up to keep you as a friend. I didn't want to lose you any more than Easton did. And I knew that once your hearts connected and you fulfilled each other's deepest desires, you would be gone. And I would remain. And then, I would be the one with an empty heart."

I wrapped my hand around the nape of my neck—a worry set deep within. I hurt for her. She'd been a soul dedicated to helping others, and her own basic needs had gone unmet as a result. It was the ultimate sacrifice, and she'd been doing it ever since they called her a witch and burned her at the stake.

"I'm *so* sorry, Becca . . . I should have done better—"

"No, don't be! I love you so much—" I began.

"No. Not for that—" she said, as the phone rang.

A chill set in, sending a shiver down my spine. The phone rang a second time, and the three of us looked at one another. Only Easton and I were uncertain of the doom that hung in the balance. The phone rang a third time, and nobody moved to pick it up.

It was then when Brooklyn said, "It's your mother . . ."

CHAPTER 14

The day was long and the night restless. Not just for me, but Easton, too. Clara had spent the day introducing Bodie to every square inch of the house. While I followed them supervising, my mind was off in a distant land. Had I really not been a Tethered Soul? All this time? My tether was born not of the cancer that stole my life but from the man who stole my heart? Had it been a symbol of our undying love? If so, it hadn't been a curse at all.

My life was cut short but nothing like the horrific events that both Easton and Brooklyn had to endure. I had time to experience friendships and a loving family. I was lucky enough to have fallen in love. And if I really thought about it . . . I had a damn good life. The funny thing was, I never knew it. Until now, that was.

It was so easy to think of all the experiences I would never have. And it was so easy to see the ill-fated existence, that I never opened my eyes to the remarkable life around me. I may never have seen it without the privilege of knowing Easton or Brooklyn. Their struggles were so real, so heartbreaking, that they thoroughly put my first life into perspective.

I'd had . . . a wonderful life until my diagnosis. And even then, the worst part was feeling alone, and I think I did that to myself.

I really had been my own worst enemy. Because life was what you made of it, and I'd been skipping out on all the things that made it worthwhile. I always thought life had to be long to be fulfilling. Or that you had to change the world in some grand way to matter. But that wasn't true at all.

I watched as Clara showed Bodie her favorite stuffed animal and I wondered if she would grow up with the perspective that I had in my first life, or if it was something I could teach her now. And as Bodie sniffed around her room, I began to wonder about Nora and how much more difficult it would be to teach her what so few knew.

That night, when Clara was fast asleep—with Bodie at the foot of her bed—I lay on Easton's chest, my eyes refusing to close for slumber. Easton's fingers trailed up and down my back as he, too, was filled with thoughts so loud he couldn't sleep. I had known for some time that I was living my last life, but this was a first for him, and I could feel the tension radiating from his skin. Maybe it was because my heart had been so tangled up with his, or maybe this was how everyone loved, but I could feel his troubles just like they were mine.

"What is it?" I asked, even though I was pretty sure I already knew.

"I'm just having a hard time with all of this. I thought

we had forever. I don't know if I believe Brooklyn or not, but I can't shake the thought that maybe, one day, you'll be leaving me."

"You don't know if you believe her?" I asked.

"She said she didn't even know if she was right. She said it was only a theory. How can I believe her when she doesn't even believe herself?" He had a valid point. But I knew how I felt inside, and that was all I needed.

"I think she's right," I said. "I've only known a few Tethered Souls before, Nora being one of them, and they were all much younger than I when they were taken. I was so conditioned to think that my life was unfair. I mean . . . it was, but, what I never realized was it had its moments, too. I met you. I fell in love. I wasn't robbed in the way that I always believed. And if I really think back, I was a lucky girl," I said, planting a kiss on his bare chest.

"You really think that?"

"I do."

"You're a better person than I."

"That's not true. Don't say that," I said.

"Beck, I don't know what's going to happen, but I don't want to lose you," he said.

"You're not going to," I said as I rolled on top of him, straddling him.

"And how can you be so sure," he asked, placing his hands on my hips.

I planted a kiss on his cheek. "Because, my heart is anchored in yours," I whispered. Then, I moved to kiss his other cheek. "And where you go, I go . . ."

He wrapped his hand around the nape of my neck,

pulling me in for a deep and long kiss. "Promise?" he asked in a breathy, heady voice.

"I promise," I said. And I meant it. I would try my hardest to stay with him wherever he may roam.

He rolled me over, moaning into my mouth. "Are you OK?" I asked, trying to see his wounds through the darkness of the late night. I felt his bandage scratch the inner part of my thigh and I lowered my knee down against the bedsheets. He nodded just before taking my breath away.

His hold a little tighter, his urgency more intense. My hands gripped tightly as my heart pounded in a way that felt fleeting. Time was slipping through our fingers, and it was more important than ever to show just how deep our love had grown.

Time had passed swiftly, the weeks coming and going with the blink of an eye. My mom's funeral was nice. It was a quiet service. Lindsay attended with the small crowd. Every now and then, she would look over her shoulder at Easton and me in the distance. She was too far away for me to read her expression, but even so, I knew she was wishing I could be there with her and my family.

It was after the service I could tell that her wheels had spun. She looked at me in a way that she never had before. At first, it worried me, but soon it became a look of comfort. And sometime after the service, she had our family over for dinner for the first time. It had been a little odd knowing that John didn't know our secrets, but it was just like when we used to have dinner with Brooklyn and Tanner. Tanner being on the outside of a very secret life we all shared. Lucky for us, John had been such a busy guy that he hardly had the time to consider all of it.

"If you don't mind, John and I would like to talk to you guys about something important," Lindsay said. Dinner was done, and the girls had run off to play in Nora's room.

"Of course!" I said, glancing at Easton.

Lindsay looked at John and took his hand in hers. She gave him a quick nod, and he replied with a wide-eyed look that I couldn't quite read. "I wanted to talk to you guys about Nora. It might come as a surprise, but she's adopted. We took Nora in when she was a baby," Lindsay said. My stomach dropped, and my eyes ticked toward Easton's. He played it much cooler than I.

"I had no idea," he said, simply.

"Yeah. I had a hysterectomy some time back because of cancerous cells."

"Oh, no!" I said.

Easton nodded, "Uh, huh."

"It's OK. We caught it super early. But the devastating part was that I couldn't get pregnant. We had always wanted to have a baby, and I was especially looking forward to taking advantage of John's 3D ultrasound pictures," Lindsay said with a nervous laugh. I chuckled along with her, equally nervous about where the conversation was going.

"Anyway, we applied for adoption. It took some time, but we were approved. One day, when I was visiting him in the hospital, this beautiful baby caught my eye. I remember she stole my heart right away. It wasn't long after that we received a call from the adoption company assigning a baby girl to us." Lindsay's eyes started to water and her voice rose several octaves. "It was her. It was Nora. I just knew it was meant to be . . ."

I felt a tug at my heart, knowing that she was meant to be ours above anyone else. That fate had twisted unconventionally to give Lindsay what she'd always wanted. And that it was I who suffered the consequences. It left a bitter taste in my mouth, and I was rendered speechless.

"And just as Nora was meant to be in our lives, we believe that your family is a part of that plan. You have become so important to us in such a short time," Lindsay said, her eyes flicking to her husband's. "Would you take Nora in, should anything happen to us?"

I stared into Lindsay's eyes, my emotions scattered like a dandelion pappus riding in the wind. It had been everything I ever wanted—both my girls under my wing. But not at the expense of my oldest friend.

"We would be honored. The girls are already best friends, and Becca nannies Nora; it would be seamless for our family to take her in. You have nothing to worry about in the off event that something happens to you prematurely," Easton said, reaching for my hand.

I looked towards John, who had somewhat of a suspicious look in his eyes. Easton had been confident and strong, and Lindsay a weeping mess. I gazed at each of them through what felt like a lens of slow motion. It was when Easton squeezed my hand that I jolted back into the present moment, remembering that I, too, needed to speak.

"Nothing would make us happier . . . I mean . . . No, not like that!" I fumbled over my words. Lindsay chuckled through her tears, and John's scowl deepened. "I mean, you have our word. We would do everything in our power to raise her"—I swallowed, my throat dry as could be—"as our own . . ." I choked out.

Lindsay covered her mouth, crying into the palm of her hand. She stood, the chair screeching along the tile behind her as she made her way to me.

"I've written your family up in our will," said John. "The papers will be recorded later this week. Let us know if you change your minds. It's no problem at all for us to amend the will at any time. Any time at all," he added, being crystal clear.

Lindsay squeezed me tight, and I patted her back, still wounded from her earlier comment. Through Lindsay's hair, I caught John shrugging as he shook Easton's hand. "They've just become so close, so fast," he said, meaning for only Easton to hear. It was clear he didn't understand what was going on between Lindsay and me, or even the girls, for that matter. And from what I gathered, he was skeptical but not necessarily opposed.

"Yeah, they're like kindred spirits—or old friends," Easton said in return.

Lindsay pulled away and wiped the tears from her cheeks. "Thank you. You don't know how much this means to me. When I saw you at the funeral, I just realized how much you're like family to me. And I want you to know that," Lindsay said, quiet enough for only us to hear. She looked back at John, beaming at him from across the dining room.

"Is he OK with this?" I asked.

"Oh, yeah. Of course," she said.

"Um, you're like family to me, too. And Nora . . . she's . . . she's . . ." I couldn't say it. I couldn't say anything that wasn't true any longer. Nora wasn't *like* family, she *was* family. "Hey, can we talk?"

Lindsay's brows came together in concern. "Yeah, is everything OK?" she asked.

"Everything's OK. But there is something I need to tell you. And it's . . . private," I said, looking back at the boys. Lindsay's gaze followed mine. She took a deep breath before nodding her head.

"Um, John?" she said.

"Yeah?"

"I forgot dessert. Becca and I are going to run out really quick to pick up some ice cream."

"Are you sure? The girls won't even notice," he said.

"Of course they will! Plus, we're celebrating!" Lindsay said. I offered a smile of encouragement.

"Well, why don't I go? You can stay here?"

"Oh no. That's OK. We'll be right back," Lindsay said, pulling me in tow. I passed Easton with lifted brows and I saw him bring his hand to his stomach nervously.

"Be back soon!" I said before turning away.

CHAPTER 15

It was s'mores ice cream, a pink plastic spoon, and my last secret. Lindsay and I sat in the parking lot of the ice cream shop with the headlights turned off and the music playing softly in the background. I dug through my ice cream, looking for a place to start. I preferred it to be a thick ribbon of marshmallow, but I had more pressing concerns at the moment.

"Are you sure you're OK with my request? I know it's a lot. And I know I'm older than you now, but I—" Lindsay said, waving her spoon around in the driver's seat.

"No! That's not it. That's not it at all." I said. A long pause stretched between us when I didn't follow up.

"Then what is?" she asked.

"I . . . I don't know how to say it," I stammered.

"Beck, just spit it out. I literally asked you to take my daughter if I die. The least you can do is talk to me about whatever's bothering you," she said, spooning her mint chip ice cream.

"OK. I'll just say it. But you have to promise me you won't get mad at me. And that things will not change between us. Because I couldn't handle that."

"What are you talking about? Nothing is changing!" Lindsay brought her hand up in question.

"Just promise me, Lindsay."

"OK. I promise. Now say it."

I took a moment. Her promise was short and sharp, not at all what I wanted to hear before saying that her adopted daughter never should have been up for adoption in the first place—that it was all an accident. "Nora . . ." I started, but fear swelled my throat shut. What if she turned on me? What if she thought I was trying to take her away? What if they moved and I never saw Nora again?

"Beck, you're starting to scare me . . ." Lindsay lowered her ice cream into her lap and laid her eyes on mine. The pressure was peaking at an all-time high.

"No, I'm sorry. That's not my intention. I'm just scared," I said.

"What about Nora?" Lindsay asked.

"Nora . . . Nora is mine," I said. It came out all wrong. It was true, but it sounded off. The words hung in the air and I watched as Lindsay tried to grasp at them.

"I don't . . . What does that mean? I don't—" She ran a hand through her hair.

I set my ice cream on the dashboard and turned to my oldest friend, remembering the worst day of my lives. "Clara was a twin. Do you remember?"

"Yeah, I remember John said it was terrible. I'm sorry, but what does that have to do with—" Lindsay's voice cut out abruptly, and her eyes wandered down to the console between us. My stomach dropped as I could see the puzzle pieces finding their counterparts behind her misty eyes. "No. No, your baby *died!*" she said. The word stung like a hot iron branding my skin.

"My baby *passed*, and on the very same day—as Tethered Souls do—she came back, for a second chance at life," I said, my voice quiet but clear.

"And you think, that your baby is Nora? That's oddly convenient, don't you think? Do you even hear yourself right now?" Lindsay scolded. It was everything I was afraid of, and it was coming at me like a tidal wave. Reckless and unrelenting.

"Didn't you think it was weird how quickly the girls took to one another?" I asked. Tears streamed down Lindsay's cheeks. "Didn't you think it's weird how you had an automatic connection to her? Above any other baby in that nursery, it was her that you felt something for. Don't you think that's odd? Or how they share the same birthday? I mean, look at me! I'm living proof that not all things end in death! And Nora is the same way!"

"Stop it! Stop it! Just stop!" she yelled, cradling her head between her hands. It was then that I realized she was just as afraid as I was.

"Lindsay . . . I know you're scared. I am too. My biggest fear right now is that you will leave me and you'll take Nora with you. I'm so afraid that I won't be able to have her in my life," I said.

"You're afraid? I wake up every day scared that some court order will take her away from me! And now you're telling me that she's yours? And you never wanted to put her up for adoption?"

"No, Lindsay, that's not what I'm saying. I mean it is true—" Lindsay cried harder.

"It's true! I never wanted any of this! But it happened, and I'm so happy that it happened with you! Could you imagine if she was adopted by another family? Or if she never had a second chance life at all? I got my baby back . . ." Tears stung the back of my eyes.

". . . And I got a daughter," Lindsay added.

I reached over the console and grabbed her hand. "We can do this, right? We can raise that beautiful girl. And she will have four loving parents. And a sister!" I said.

"I don't know, Beck . . ." Lindsay pulled her hand away.

"What do you mean?"

"I don't want her to know that you're her biological mother, if that's even what you are. That will jeopardize *my* relationship with her. I'm her *real* mother!" she said. It stung once more, and I closed my eyes briefly to get through the pain.

Then, with everything I had, I said, "Thank you for raising her when I couldn't."

It sent not only Lindsay over the top, but me too. We cried together, both mothers afraid of parenting. I wiped my nose on the back of my hand and caught a glimpse of Lindsay doing the same. When I saw how much pain we had put ourselves through, I began to laugh. We were best friends who both loved Nora deeply. What was there to cry about? At some point, Lindsay and I found ourselves laughing together.

"You spilled your ice cream!" I shrieked. Lindsay picked up her bowl and tried to wipe her pant leg with a napkin, and the ice cream spread down her jeans. We both laughed harder.

"I know. I'm a train wreck," she said.

"No, you're not. I'm the wreck."

"I'm the one that's afraid you're trying to take my daughter away from me ..."

"What? No, I'd never do that. I'm scared you're going to take her from *me!*" I said.

Lindsay looked at me, the lines in her forehead prominent. "I wouldn't do that, either," she said in all seriousness. "I mean, I just called you guys over to ask if you would take her if we died in some terrible w—oh, sorry, I didn't mean—"

"No, no. It's OK," I said.

"All I'm saying is that I'd never take her away from you. Whether she's Clara's sister or not, I'm not going to lose you again. You're like family to me," she said.

"Then it's settled. We'll just keep everything the same. I'll be Nora's 'nanny,' " I air quoted, "and she will just think we're close family friends."

"I'm OK with that," Lindsay said.

"And you know, if you ever want to tell her, we can do it together," I said.

"Deal," Lindsay said, offering me a small smile.

"Deal." I picked my ice cream off the dashboard and sighed. "It's melted."

"At least it's not all down your leg," she said, trying one more time to clean up the mess. Ultimately, she crumpled up the napkin and threw it in the backseat. "Hey, Beck?" I looked up from my melted s'mores, and something in her eyes worried me.

"What is it?" I asked.

"Can we get a DNA test? Not because I don't believe you or anything . . . Although, I think we can agree that would be perfectly just, if I didn't. But more or less, just for me to see it. I think it would really help wrap my mind around the idea," she said.

"Of course. Do you think we can do it secretively?" I asked.

"Yeah, nobody needs to know. I think Nora will cooperate."

"OK, then let's do it," I said, suddenly afraid that maybe I'd been wrong the whole time. But I couldn't be. *Could I?*

"Well, we should get back before the guys start to wonder what happened to us," Lindsay said, pulling down her mirror. "God, I look like death!" she said. I pulled down my mirror and moaned before trying to wipe away the black mascara that had settled in the crevices under my eyes.

We rode back to Lindsay's house, mostly in silence. I worried that I had made the whole thing up in my head and that the only piece of concrete information that I had been counting on was that the girls shared a birthdate. It was odd but not impossible for two friends to share a birthday. But then I remembered her glacier eyes. The icy blue that reminded me so much of Easton, and I knew in my heart that the DNA test would show she was our own flesh and blood.

"Hey, Lindsay . . . There's one more thing we should discuss while we're alone," I said.

"Oh, shit, Beck. Honestly, I can't take anymore!" Lindsay glanced at me sideways before returning her gaze to the traffic lights just down the road. The neon green light lit the side of her face.

"It's nothing like that. But have you ever heard Nora talking about the lights?" I asked.

Lindsay raised her arm, and her hair was standing on end. "You're really freaking me out, Everly! I'm covered in chills! She talks about them all the time. Are you trying to tell me that's some weird Tethered Soul thing and not a normal little kid thing? I knew it wasn't normal!"

I smiled, pushing her arm down to her side. "Well, it's no normal little kid thing . . ."

"Dammit! Why do you have to do this to me?" Lindsay whined. She never liked scary stories or anything she couldn't see in the daylight.

I laughed at her. "I'm not doing anything! It's just that she can see things."

"No!" Lindsay protested.

"—Weird things that normal people can't. Things like emotion. She can see the pain that people carry. It looks like a weird glow of hot embers. And she can see love, too. And that's the lights she always chases when she's with Clara," I said.

Lindsay placed one hand over her heart, and her chin wobbled back and forth. "That's the most beautiful thing, I've ever heard," her voice cutting out. Lindsay nodded, deep in thought. "She sees most of her lights when she's around Clara," she agreed.

I smiled, happy that Lindsay and I ended what could have been a disastrous discussion in the same positive place. "It's because they're sisters," I said.

"Sisters," she whispered, deep in thought.

When we walked back into the house joking with one another, we were taken aback by the guys' expressions.

"What?" I asked.

"Good lord, where did you go to buy ice cream? I thought you'd never come back," John said.

Easton laughed nervously. "You got ice cream, right?" he said, looking down at our empty hands. My jaw gaped open. We had forgotten to get the girls' ice cream.

"Oh, um, they were all out," Lindsay said, unconvincingly.

"Is that ice cream on your pants?" John pointed to Lindsay's leg. Her face flushed, caught in the lie, and all I could do was laugh at her. I grabbed her elbow and hid my face behind her back. And I laughed even harder when she stuck to her guns and continued on with her story, even though nobody was buying it.

Finally, she ended the fabrication with some extravagant story about how we bought ice cream but ended up dropping it in the parking lot and we were too embarrassed to go back inside and buy more. At which point, John gave up on his suspicious endeavor and threw his hands in the air, all but giving up. Lindsay never had to say what really happened, but I imagined it wasn't difficult to piece together.

The night was late, and Lindsay and I were beyond tired. When I scooped Clara up in my arms, she fought me tooth and nail, not wanting to go home.

"No! Can't she stay? Please!" Nora asked Lindsay.

"Not tonight, but soon, OK?" Lindsay said.

"It's not fair! She always takes the sparkling lights with her when she goes!" Nora stomped her foot, and Lindsay shot me a look, her face pale as a ghost.

John sighed, batting his hand dismissively. "She's got this thing. It's like an imaginary friend, but she says they're lights. We've been trying to ignore it, hoping it will go away when she sees we don't pay it any attention," he said, leaning into Easton. Lindsay bit her lip, looking between John, Easton, and me.

"Hey, Nora . . . we all have to get a good night's sleep tonight, but I promise you we will have so many sparkles next time you come over that you won't know what to do with them all!" I said. The corners of Nora's pout curved ever so slightly as she nodded.

"But I never get to see them! Why should she be the only one to play with them?" Clara yelled out. I brushed the hair from my face and looked at Lindsay with exhaustion. If it wasn't one, it was the other, and nothing was ever fair.

"Come on, Clara." I picked her up, ignoring her rant. I'd heard it before, and I had spent countless nights worrying over it, but when I said goodnight to Lindsay, it was clear it was her first time understanding the depth of my family affairs. Her eyes trailed from mine to Clara as she pulled Nora in close. She rested her hands firmly on her shoulders.

"We'll be in touch," John said, waving us goodbye. I blew the girls a kiss, and Easton wrapped his hand around my shoulder as I hugged Clara to my hip.

The door closed behind us on our way out, and I took a long, deep sigh of relief. "You know Clara, some people can *see* sparkles, but you know what? You have the ability to *feel* them . . . right, here," I said, patting her heart as we walked down the Faye's driveway.

CHAPTER 16

$\mathcal{A}$ crack of thunder rattled deep inside my old, timeworn bones, scaring me and Tiny Tommy alike. The storm hadn't let up the entire morning. And I was worried about Easton when he slipped out after our time on the porch. I knew he needed space. Time to gather himself, find his strength. Because I knew he wouldn't want me to see him crumble any more than he already had. He didn't want me to worry in that way. But I worried now because he had gone out in the storm.

I picked up the leather-bound journal I had been working on for the last several months since receiving my diagnosis. Whenever I had a memory—something worth sharing—I jotted it down. The book was nearly full, and by the end of the day, it would be complete. And although I had written nearly two hundred pages in the journal, it was the last four that would be by far the most difficult. I had written goodbye letters before, but that didn't make writing them today any easier.

I wrote to Clara, telling her what a gift she had been in my life and how honored I had been to raise her. I pleaded with her to remember me with a smile. It always crushed me to see the guilt that plagued survivors long after the passing of a loved one. Being a loved one myself and having the fortune to come back to see it firsthand was not a pleasurable experience. I may venture to say that their sadness was worse than the death itself. Although I never went to my own funeral, I had seen the damage that unfolds after the departure. A broken heart takes time, and I let her know that was OK, too. I wrote that sometimes we lose someone special. It's inevitable, really. I knew how deeply it hurt but that one day, she'd be able to laugh again, love again, and live again. She may not get a second chance like I did, and possibly the best thing she could ever do was not count on it. Make this the one life in which she shined her brightest. And to remember, all things lost can be found. She just needed to know where to look.

And as for me, I told her she could find me in the gentle ocean breeze, the warm summer sky, and the wind beneath a dragonfly's wings. I told her I would look out for her children and grandchildren, and that I'd do everything in my power to warm her heart when she needed her mother's love.

I licked my finger and turned the page. I took a moment to reflect, as my mind moved slower these days. I found myself gazing out the window at the rolling sheets of rain and cloudy condensation covering the windows. I pulled a cardigan over my shoulders and began my letter to Nora. I could never be sure, but it was my gut that told me Nora would take after her father and that her life fulfillment wouldn't be earned on the second try. I knew she had a long road ahead of her, but I promised that I would help in any way I could. I encouraged her to take chances and open her heart. I wrote that pain is growth and that it would always be better to love with loss than to never love at all. She needed to believe that deep down in her heart of hearts if she wanted to earn her rite of passage. I knew she would one day.

I leaned back in my chair and remembered a particular moment in time that led me to believe Nora was in it for the long haul. She was a teenager in high school. The girls looked so beautiful in their winter formal dresses. I remembered taking pictures of them with their dates outside in the rose garden.

The air was crisp, and the girls were anxious. Nora was dating a perfect gentleman—a favorite of all the parents. Landon treated her with such respect, and I believed he loved her. She was easy to fall for. Many of the boys she hung around had puppy love deep in their eyes. Nora, on the other hand . . . she never opened herself up to Landon's compassion. And sometimes I wondered if she even noticed it at all.

"Just one more. Trent's eyes were closed," I said. Trent huffed before wrapping his arm around Clara's waist again. Trent was a good guy, but I couldn't help but compare him to Landon. And I always hoped Clara would find a boy that treated her like Landon did Nora. I snapped another picture. It wasn't perfect, but I knew the kids' patience was wearing thin. I waved them on.

"Can we go now?" Clara asked. She always took on Trent's impatience and wore it like a cloak of anxiety. I never liked him for her, but she swore she saw something in him that no one else had. I took her word for it. I had no other choice.

"Yeah, you can go. Have so much fun! Take lots of pictures! And call me if—" The car door slammed. Nobody was listening to me. My head fell to the side, and Easton wrapped his arm around my shoulder. At least I had him.

"Goodbye!" yelled Landon out the window. I smiled, finally settled. We watched the car pull out of the driveway, and I hoped they would have a memorable night. I never imagined they'd be coming home so upset.

Several hours had passed when the girls came home—alone. Easton and I were in the middle of a heated poker game, and I had just uncorked a bottle of wine. I jumped when the front door slammed and the girls came barreling in, arguing.

"Wow, what's going on?" I looked at my watch, trying to focus on the tiny numbers. "You're early," I said.

"Well, that's what happens when Clara gets dumped," Nora said. I couldn't understand why Nora was angry about that.

"You got dumped, honey?" I asked Clara. Her eyes were red and puffy, telling me everything I needed to know. She said nothing, only came bounding into my arms, crying. "Oh, Clara, I'm so sorry!" I said, stroking her hair. "I'm so sorry, honey!"

Nora stood by the doorway, arms crossed over her chest. When Clara pulled away, she excused herself to take a hot bath. She didn't say one word to Nora as she disappeared. Easton cleaned up the cards, and I took my wine to the kitchen. "Um, Mrs. Green? My car is at home. Do you think you could give me a ride?" Nora asked.

"Oh, sure honey!" I said. I turned my attention to Easton, who had adopted my freshly poured glass of wine. "I'll be back soon," I said, gathering my bag. He nodded. I looked down the hall toward Clara's room as we walked out of the house. I knew she was upset, and I figured she would be even more upset now that Nora wasn't staying over.

"Is everything alright? Sounds like you guys had a rough night," I said, starting the ignition.

"It was a disaster! I feel terrible for Clara, but she kind of did it to herself. She never listens to me!" Nora said.

"So, what happened?" I asked.

"Well, Trent is a dirtbag—that's what happened. He used her. I'd been telling her all along that he wasn't *the one*. And she didn't listen."

"The one?" I asked with trepidation.

Nora fell quiet, which was a rarity for her. "You know . . . *the one* . . ." She said.

My stomach dropped as I recalled the tears in Clara's eyes when she ran into my arms. "Oh no . . ."

"Yeah, and then he dumped her! What an asshole!" Nora said, tongue sharp. "I saw it all over him. His vibe was weird and jagged. I didn't like the way it sat on his skin, and it always seemed like he changed her vibe, too.

But not in a good way. She had the lights for him, but he never did for her. Or anyone, for that matter. That boy is incapable of love! I can't believe she fell for it!"

"Huh . . ." I nodded, knowing that I had never liked Trent, either. Not that I ever saw jagged edges on his frame, but a mother knows unexplainable things in her own right. Nora was talented when it came to seeing the lights, but for whatever reason, I rarely saw them. And I wished I had known before so that I could warn my daughter of the love that she gave but didn't receive. "And you told her all of that?" I asked.

"I told her countless times," she said.

I thought about what she said about the lights, and I wondered if she could see her own, or if her emotions clouded her own manifestation, making it incapable for her to see. "And do you have lights for Landon?" I asked.

"Me? No. Landon is just a boy . . . He's cute though, right?" she joked.

"He's very handsome, but you don't have that connection with him?"

"Um, no. He could vanish tomorrow and I couldn't care less."

"Well, honey, you have to be careful. I think he might have more significant feelings for you. You don't want to hurt him," I said, worried about the impressionable heart of his youth.

"He's great! I like having him around. But, I just . . . He doesn't know anything about me. Like, I'd never tell him I could see emotions and whatever. We don't really talk in that way. We just go to parties together . . . I've actually been thinking that I don't really want a boyfriend anymore. And now that Clara is single, maybe I'll break it off with Landon, too. He felt really bad about what happened to Clara. God, if I didn't know any better, I'd say he has feelings for Clara!" There Nora was. The one I'd come to know and love. The one who spoke everything on her mind no matter how fast those thoughts were moving.

"Oh! Well, that would be a mess, huh? Why do you think you haven't given Landon a chance to get to know you?"

"Oh, I don't know. Nobody knows me like your family does. I just feel like people don't get me. So why even bother, you know?" She shrugged and looked out the window. She looked so pretty in her dress, and I wished she had the confidence to show the world just how special she really was. But Nora was good at putting up walls. Her exterior was hard as nails, and sometimes icy, too. Only I knew it was an act. A way of protecting herself from a broken heart like Clara had experienced after the winter formal.

". . . Honey, if you don't have a connection with the boy, the sooner the better, so you don't lead him on. He's such a great guy. I'd hate to see him get hurt beyond what's necessary," I said.

"You're right. There . . . Done."

"What's done?" I asked, looking over at Nora. Her eyes focused on her phone.

"I just told Landon that we aren't right for each other." Nora's face glowed from the light of her cell, and not an ounce of remorse reflected in her eyes.

"Just now?" I asked, shocked.

"You know what? It's for the better. I never loved him like Clara loved that dirtbag, Trent. And maybe now Clara and I can look for new boys together." Nora shrugged, unbuckling. "Thanks for the ride, Mrs. Green!" she said, hopping out of the car.

I watched in disbelief. That poor boy. Nora was a heartbreaker, and I feared it stemmed from feeling like an outcast her whole life. She didn't know that she was a Tethered Soul, but she knew she was unlike others. And I could only believe she knew that she didn't quite fit in with her family either. Sometimes, it looked a little like resentment toward Clara for having the family she felt most accepted with. Other times, it looked like she was cruel and selfish. But I knew her heart, and it was made of gold. I did what I could to make her feel loved. And I knew that Lindsay and John did, too. So, there was no shortage of love in Nora's life, but being an outsider in her own home and amongst her peers must have been a deep ocean of turmoil for her. And I didn't think she was handling it all that well.

When I got home, I gave Easton a quick peck on the cheek. I told him not to wait up and that I'd be having a girls' night in Clara's room.

"Clara?" I asked softly as I opened her door. She lay on her side, hair wet and eyes still red. "Are you OK?" I asked.

When she didn't respond, I curled up behind her and hugged her tightly. Her body quaked with silent cries, and I held her through the regret of giving herself to the wrong person.

"I loved him, Mom! I don't understand . . ." she cried.

"I know you didn't understand him, but he was special. He cared so much about his little sister. You never saw that. And he tried really hard to get passing grades, even though it didn't come naturally to him. He worked really hard. You didn't see it like I did," she said, defending him still.

I wanted to tell her that she was so young that she didn't yet know what love was, but I knew what she felt for Trent was real to her. She had such a kind heart that she would see the best in anyone that she looked at for long enough. "He just wasn't the right one. Shh, I know it hurts," I said, soothing her as much as I could. "Heartbreak hurts."

"Why? Why does it feel like this? I'm so stupid. How could I not have seen it?" she murmured.

"It's hard. Our emotions cloud a lot of our better judgment—"

"But Nora has the best boyfriend in the world! He's so caring and thoughtful, and she treats him like shit! I don't get it!"

There wasn't much I could say, but I could hold her. She went on and on about how Nora had everything she didn't and how she ended up with the short end of the stick. I wanted to tell her that Nora saw it just the same way, but I only listened.

It was after Clara fell asleep that I knew Nora would need more than one lifetime to get her heart straight. And I couldn't help but wonder if she had known the truth about being a Tethered Soul—and our past lives—if she would have grown up with such a bulletproof exterior? And would she have needed it, had she known just who she was?

Little did I know that the time when she would find out exactly who she was and how she came to be was just around the corner.

CHAPTER 17

The following year, when the girls were seventeen and fighting for their independence, they took it too far one evening when they failed to come home. I was used to the unanswered calls and the stretching of curfew, but this was different. It was an hour later than I expected to see Clara at home, and she hadn't been answering her phone. By the second hour, I called Nora to no avail. It was unusual that neither of the girls would answer. When I spoke to Lindsay, she had said that she thought the girls were staying at our house, but that was never the case. Not that I knew of anyhow.

Three hours into the silence and I was on the phone with Easton. He had been at work all evening, which most likely gave him better access to finding the girls. He was surprised when I said I hadn't heard from either of them, but he wasn't as worried as I'd become. He did what he could to reassure me that everything would be OK. And he promised to look into it. He had special equipment at the station for tracking cell phones and credit cards, all of which he'd used to check up on the girls before. By the time I'd gotten off the call, I felt better about the expected outcome of the evening.

But when Easton had called to say he found nothing, worry stirred in my chest. He said he checked the location of the girls' cell phones, but the last known location pinged from their high school a little after lunch hour. "The phone must have died. Do you know if it was charged?" Easton asked.

"She's really good at keeping it charged. Do you really think that both of their cell phones would die at the same time?" I asked.

"Well—"

"And why haven't they come home?"

"Right. It doesn't add up. Did Clara say anything? Any after-school plans? New friends? Anything you can think of?" Easton asked.

"No. Nothing!"

"Did you talk to Lindsay yet?"

"Yes, and she said that Nora told her she was staying at our house tonight," I said.

"But she wasn't?"

"No, Clara never mentioned that."

"OK, well, it sounds like maybe they turned their phones off and went to a party or something. Just stay by your phone, and I'll keep my eye out," Easton said, calmer than I would have liked. I didn't need him to worry like I had been, but I didn't want the anxious storm in my chest to be invalidated, either.

I couldn't understand what would have happened, and at school no less. Why would they turn their phones off at the same time after lunch hour? It's not like a party would start in the middle of the school day. Unless it had? Unless they ditched? But it was a Tuesday. My mind ran wild, trying to fit the puzzle pieces together. But there were too many missing pieces to make out any semblance of a picture.

Easton drove the streets, looking for the girls after his shift had ended. I sat on the sofa, my cell phone in hand. I had worried myself sick watching the minutes tick by. I made a list of hospitals and called them all. Every time I was placed on hold, I would feel my heart kick out. And every time the operator came back on the line with no known patient, I was relieved. No news was good news, I told myself. But it was the no news that left a gaping hole that I desperately needed to be filled.

It was about two in the morning when my knee began bouncing relentlessly. My cell phone was clutched in my hand. Volume on high. I knew Clara was a happy girl, and that she would never choose to run away or worry me unnecessarily. That's why the pit of my stomach had filled with doom, and my knee wouldn't stop from vaulting. Because maybe it wasn't her choice at all.

When I couldn't take it any longer, I did what I swore I'd never do. And hadn't done so, until now. I called Brooklyn. I called, looking for answers from her unconscious premonitions. It was a cheat in my book. I didn't think it was right for me to ask, but in my moment of weakness—my back against the wall—I had no other choice. At first, Brooklyn didn't answer. But by the third try, I'd finally woken her up.

"Becca? Do you know what time it is?" she answered the phone.

"I need your help Brooklyn," I pled.

"What? What is it?" she asked.

"It's the girls. They haven't come home, and neither one of them is answering their phones!" I said.

A moment passed where all I could hear was the deep breaths of Brooklyn over the phone. And then she asked, "Is it October?"

"Yes?"

"And the girls are seventeen, right?"

"Yes!"

"OK. Yeah, they ran away," Brooklyn said sleepily.

"What!" I shrieked.

"Uh, huh."

I sat on the other end of the line, rattled with disbelief. How could my sweet Clara run away? More importantly, *why* would she run away?

"Hey, Becca?" Brooklyn asked.

"Yeah?"

"I'm going to go back to bed now. They're going to be alright. Just try not to lose it, OK?" she said.

"What? Are you serious? That's it?" I asked.

"What did I say? Hold it together. Oh, and Becca?"

"Yeah?"

"Show them some sympathy . . ." It was the last thing Brooklyn said and the furthest thing from my mind.

When Lindsay was finished with her night shift at

Sunny Hill Assisted Living, she came directly to my house. It was still too early for the sun to rise, but I made a pot of coffee anyhow. She was worried sick, as I had been, but I told her what Brooklyn had said. She was fascinated by Brooklyn's story. One I vowed not to speak of to anyone, but since I had been breaking all the rules tonight, I let it slide. Plus, it gave us something to talk about. A much-needed distraction.

Easton called with updates, though they weren't much to go by. "A girl seen in the parking lot of a shopping mall" or "teenagers pulled over for speeding down the highway." None of them turned out to be our girls, until he had a lead he was going to check on that was an hour away. He thought it was worth the drive, and I encouraged him to look into it. The surveillance feed was pixilated, but he'd been going off a feeling, and I always encouraged those.

Lindsay and I spat speculations until the sun rose, casting a warm hue in the sky. And when Easton called to say he had found them and they were on their way home, my relief was strong but short-lived. Soon after the call, my relief turned straight to white-hot anger, and I wasn't the only one. Lindsay had been just as angry as me. I didn't know their story, but I knew how afraid I had felt for the past twelve hours, and I was going to punish them until they knew my pain.

When Easton walked through the door with the girls in tow, Lindsay and I ran to them, hugging them tightly out of pure instinct. Only, neither of the girls reciprocated that love. Clara could have been a block of ice pulled close to my chest and I'd never have known the difference. Her body was stiff and cold.

I pulled back, trying to look into her eyes, but she refused to acknowledge me. My anger melted into worry as Easton sighed with a heavy look of empathy. How could he empathize with the girls after all they'd put us through? I couldn't understand.

"Where have you been?" Lindsay demanded.

"Do you have any idea how worried we were?" I added. But our words had fallen on deaf ears.

"We need to have a talk. All of us," Easton said, locking up his gun. "I'll be right back." Then, he headed to the bedroom to change out of his uniform. The girls didn't speak. Their eyes were glued to the floor. Maybe it was the lack of sleep or maybe it was the sting of secrets, but the air was frigid and their hearts cold.

"What is going on?" Lindsay asked. Nobody answered. The girls made their way to the sofa, and I shook my head in frustration. When Easton returned, we sat down, three to two. Three parents directly across from the two misfits who had stayed out all night. Running from nothing but the unconditional love that we had all given them. And it was clear they were prepared for a fight.

"I picked them up in Winchester—" Easton began.

"Winchester!" I barked.

"They were using cash on the local bus transportation, so we couldn't track them. They were running away," Easton confirmed. The girls looked guilty and maybe even a little regretful. Lindsay had been surprised that Brooklyn's forecast was correct.

"I had a buddy pick them up on surveillance. We're lucky, as their next stop would have been the city." I gasped, thinking of my girls in the city, alone, and in the middle of the night. It was a dangerous place—one of the worst in terms of crime.

"What do you have to say for yourselves?" I asked them. It was no surprise that Nora was the one to speak up first.

"Us? What do *we* have to say for ourselves? Why don't *you* tell *us* what you've been hiding all these years?" Nora said, with one eyebrow raised and a smoldering stare.

I opened my mouth to protest, but remembered what Brooklyn had said about showing sympathy. I didn't know how much the girls had discovered about our secret past, but I knew it was time for our surrender.

CHAPTER 18

I looked to my right at Lindsay, worried, but she was far more worried than I. Her eyes glassed over, and her forehead was perspiring. Easton, to my left, encouraged me to continue with a curt nod. "Clara?" I asked, hoping she hadn't shut me out just yet.

"Do you know what we did in school today?" Clara asked. I looked at Lindsay, but she didn't know any more than I did. "We reviewed the DNA tests we took at the beginning of the semester." My stomach dropped, and Lindsay let out a shudder. Her head went down into the palms of her hands.

"We will never forgive you for this," Nora said, not just to Lindsay but to Easton and me as well. "We only have one question for you guys," she said.

I took a deep breath, knowing that the conversation should have come a long time ago but that it was Lindsay's deepest desire to keep it secret. I knew how I felt about secrets. They were destructive, deceptive, and sometimes cruel. But if Lindsay allowed me to be part of Nora's life, I would have taken that secret to my grave.

"We will answer any and all of your questions. Together," I said.

"We're sisters?" Clara asked.

I nodded, ever so slightly. But when the girls continued to glare at me, I answered in a full-bodied voice. "Yes. You are."

"*Why* did you do this to us?" Clara asked.

"*Why* did you give me away?" asked Nora, tone cutting.

I had trouble swallowing the lump in my throat. I looked at Lindsay, giving her an opportunity to speak, but she was melting down. "Why don't you take this one, honey?" I asked Easton. I knew it was unfair, but he was the best suited. His face was void of stress, and only slight tiredness hung in the corners of his eyes. If Easton excelled at any one thing in all of his lives, it would be finding strength in the most vulnerable of times.

"We never gave you away, Nora. It was an accident—" Easton began.

Lindsay spoke for the first time since the girls sat down across from us. "No! You don't have to do that. You don't need to protect me or John. We need to tell Nora the truth."

I looked to Easton, who was in the middle of a fabrication that would last a lifetime.

"Tell me what truth?" Nora demanded.

"All of it? Do you think it's best?" Easton said, huddled behind my back.

"For Nora, it is," Lindsay said, behind me.

"But for Clara, do you think it's best she knows, too?" he asked.

"What the hell Mom? I can hear you!" Nora spat.

I saw the problem that lay before us clear as day. Nora most likely grew up feeling like an outsider with her gifts of sight. She was different than her family but comfortable with ours. And now, as the truth unfolded, Nora would feel accepted for once in her life. And she deserved that. But it was Clara who would pay the price. She would swap places with her sister and become the girl who didn't fit in. She would know that both her parents and sister were tethered while she was not. I didn't want to do that to her. But it was the truth, and they deserved to know the facts.

"No more lies. She's going to find out, anyway. These girls can't keep a secret," I said.

"Mom? What? Just tell us," Clara called out. Easton and Lindsay straightened, facing the girls once more, prepared for whatever might come our way.

"It's true. Nora is your sister. But we never knew that until you two became best friends in kindergarten," I said.

"So, you gave one up for adoption, and kept the other?" Clara asked.

"No," I said.

"She basically gave me away because my mom couldn't have kids. How much did you sell me for?" Nora scowled.

"I didn't sell you!" I rose to my feet. My chest burned like a blade had pierced into it. Easton grabbed my arm and pulled me back down. I sat begrudgingly. "When you died, it was the worst thing that had ever happened to me!" I said, breathless.

"Wow. OK, what your mother is trying to say is—"

"I died?!"

"Stop! Everybody stop!" Easton's deep voice silenced the room. "This will be easier if I tell the story from start to finish. You can ask questions when I'm done. Deal?" Everyone looked around the room, and not a single word was issued.

"There is a special gene inside our DNA, right? You've been learning about DNA . . . That gene can be flipped if something terribly unjust happens to you at a very young age. It has to be when fate bends and twists in ways it was never supposed to. And sometimes, for the greater good, a life is stolen. And when this happens, the gene of the person whose life was taken gets flipped. And that's when the person is born again. This happened to Nora when she was stillborn." Easton steepled his chin, and the girls gawked at us parents in disbelief.

"So, to answer the first question, we never gave you away. And your second question . . . yes, you died, when you were little. But you were reborn, and we never knew. Then the Fayes adopted you since they couldn't bear their own child. We have been so lucky to have since found you. And we have been working with the Faye family as much as possible to incorporate you into both families," Easton said. Lindsay and I nodded in agreement and I patted Easton's leg.

"How did you know I was Clara's sister if I was adopted?" Nora asked, still skeptical.

"Well, for starters, the lights—"

Nora clapped her hands and jumped to her feet. "I knew

it! I knew I wasn't crazy!" she said. Clara slouched back into the sofa.

"And you shared a bond unlike anything I had seen before the instant you met your sister," I added.

"We do look a lot alike," Clara said beneath her breath. The girls looked similar when they were children, but now it was obvious they were twins. People commented all the time about it. It was surprising they hadn't figured it out until now. Besides Nora's dark hair and blue eyes, Clara and she looked almost identical. Nora was somewhat taller but not by much.

"You're twins," I said. And it was the first positive breakthrough we had. Both girls smirked, looking at one another. Lindsay wilted beside me as she tried to stifle her sobs. The girls held hands, and I noticed Nora's eyes lift just above Clara's head.

"So why didn't you take me back?" Nora asked of me.

"I . . . . I couldn't. I couldn't do that to you or to your parents. They're such good people, and you had already spent six years under their roof. I thought it would be too disruptive. And to be honest with you girls, the whole genetic thing is really, really rare. So rare, that most people in the world have never heard of it," I said.

"Then how did you hear about it?" Nora asked.

"It happened to—"

"Wait . . . you said you saw the lights, too," Nora said.

"Yes," I admitted.

"So how exclusive are we talking here? Have you all had the gene switched?" she asked.

"No, not all of us. Easton and I have, and Brooklyn, too.

It's so secret that John doesn't even know about it. Most people wouldn't understand. It's probably best if you keep it quiet," I said.

"Yeah—" Clara started.

"What if we don't?" Nora questioned.

"Well, take it from me," Easton said. "You won't have many friends if you tell them you've had multiple lives."

The girls frowned, and Clara looked at Nora with concern. "Maybe you shouldn't say anything?" she said.

"You guys can't be serious," Nora's voice rose again. She must have felt like we were pulling the wool over her eyes, and I understood where she was coming from. It was difficult to grasp the impossible as sincerity. Lindsay would have never known had she not recognized me.

"Would you rather we told you there was a mix-up at the hospital?" I asked. It was the very lie I had planned on spinning, and how Easton had begun. I figured I wasn't the only one.

Nora shook her head, clearly frustrated with the entire event. I knew she didn't believe us, but it felt better knowing that there was a foundation of truth laid down before us. I planned to show her the plaque on the bridge one day where Easton's and my name rest. I would show the girls our graves and tell them stories of not only their grandpa but their pop, too. We would be as open as possible, no matter how difficult it would be to face.

"So, what happens now?" Clara asked.

I looked between Easton and Lindsay, whose eyes were swollen and filled with worry. "We keep going . . ." I said.

"Let me be the one to tell your father," Lindsay asked

Nora.

"That I'm Clara's sister? Or that I'm some rare genetic mutation?" she asked.

"Well, for now, the sister part. I have a feeling he's going to be quite upset with me, as you are. But let's keep the mutation thing to ourselves until I find a way for him to understand. Your father doesn't do well with belief. He needs proof, and I'm afraid I don't have that right now," she said.

"Well, they have the DNA test. This is going to get messy since he delivered Clara and knows what happened to Molly," I said to Lindsay.

"Who's Molly?" Nora asked.

"That's um . . . that's what your name would have been if you stuck around a little longer," I said. Nora's lip pulled up on the left side. From the looks of it, she was glad she hadn't stuck around.

"Can we go home? It's eight in the morning, and I haven't slept," she said.

"Yeah, go home. I think that's enough for one night. Or morning," I shrugged.

The girls hugged one another but didn't want to separate. They whispered amongst themselves. "Can I go to Nora's?" Clara asked. And as much as I wanted them both to stay, I nodded. I knew if the girls stayed at our house, Lindsay would go home devastated.

"Sure honey. I'm glad you two are home safe. I love you girls," I said. And my heart broke when neither of them said it back. Betrayal was a nasty road to travel, and I hoped it would be a quick path for our family.

CHAPTER 19

The girls healed as time unraveled, and eventually, things went back to normal. The only change that I could see was that the girls had a stronger relationship. They weren't just best friends anymore but sisters—*twins*. They felt the shift that came with knowing the truth. Nora had been a little leery of Easton and me, and I gathered that was because she didn't fully believe the story we'd spun. I feared she still worried I had given her up for adoption. And I didn't blame her for having trouble accepting she'd lived another life before this one.

But there was a switch in Nora's eyes after I showed the girls our memorial plaque on the bridge. The change was so pronounced, it echoed in Clara's face as well. We spent a long time there answering questions, and all three of us came back sunburnt. Still, I never felt fully accepted by Nora in the way a mother should. I told myself it would take her years or maybe even lives to open up to the idea of me being her mother. Especially if she took after Easton in so many ways. I was patient.

But on one special morning—not any morning, but the first Mother's Day since the girls found out the truth—I lay awake, eyes closed as the smell of bacon wafted through the air. Indistinct sounds of clacking and clanking came from the kitchen, and tiny voices could be heard through the walls. I rolled onto my back and stretched contently, the bedsheets like silk across my skin. My eyes fluttered open and adjusted to the morning light. It was then, when not only Clara walked through the bedroom door holding a plate of bacon, eggs, and toast but Nora too, holding a mug of coffee.

It was my first mother's day with both of my girls, and in that moment, I had never felt more honored. I sat up in bed, and a smile stretched across my face that lifted well into my eyes. "Good morning, girls," I said, my voice groggy.

"Happy Mother's Day!" Clara said.

"Good morning," Nora said.

Clara placed the hot breakfast on my lap, and Nora set the mug down on my nightstand. My stomach grumbled at the sight and smell of the bacon below. The girls sat down on the edge of the bed as I bit into the salty bacon. "It's so good. Thank you, girls. You have no idea how much this means to me. But Nora, won't your mom be upset that you're not with her this morning?" I asked.

"Oh, she's working, so Clara and I were going to surprise her at work later today," she said.

"Oh, that's right."

"Can I have some?" Clara asked.

"Yes, help yourself!" I offered, lifting my plate towards both the girls. In one quick swoop, the bacon had vanished. Next was the toast. And before I knew it, the plate was clean, and the girls were giggling just like they had when they were kids. I held my coffee close, the warmth rising under my nose.

"Um, well . . . we got you something," Clara said.

"You did?" I said, smiling.

"Yeah, both of us," Nora said, tucking her hair behind her ear. She pulled a little silver box topped with a bow from the pocket of her hooded sweatshirt and handed it to me.

"Oh, I love things that come in tiny boxes!" I said. I took the gift from Nora, whose eyes were a deeper blue than I had been used to. I untied the bow and lifted the lid off the box. Inside, nestled in white velvet, was a pair of earrings. Small studs that dropped down into a beautifully polished tiger's eye. They were both unique and absolutely perfect for the occasion. "I love them!" I exclaimed, reaching over to hug each of the girls. "Thank you, so much!"

"Happy Mother's Day, Mom," Clara said, wrapping her arms around me.

"Yeah, Happy Mother's Day," Nora said. Her embrace was anything but present. It had meant the world to me that she wanted to celebrate Mother's Day with me, but I couldn't help but want more. I wanted her to engage. I wanted her to look at me. And I wanted her to hug me so tight that I could feel her love. But she had done none of those things since she found out she was my daughter, and

I could argue that we once had a better relationship when I had only been her best friend's mom.

"We saw those, and we knew they were just as special and unique as you were. It was between those and these other ones, but we picked the tiger's eye because we'd never seen anything like them before." Clara took the box from me and removed the earrings one by one, placing them in the palm of my hand. I didn't need a mirror to slip them into my lobes, but I stood to look at them dangle once they were secured.

"They're beautiful," I said. The girls smiled, and Clara picked up the empty plate from the unmade bed.

"Well, we're going to meet Kayla and Kyndal at the coffee shop this morning if you don't mind."

"No, not at all. Go have some fun," I said, still admiring the earrings in the mirror.

"OK. I'm just going to shower really quick, and then we can take off," Clara said. I smiled at her when she walked out of my bedroom and wondered if it had been some sort of setup to leave Nora behind. Her eyes were still down— always down. The pink of her cheeks came out, and I could tell that she was growing nervous. It was the last thing I wanted for her.

"Oh, honey . . . what's wrong?" I asked. Her back quaked several times before she couldn't hold it in any longer. She crumbled before me, falling into my lap. "It's OK . . . what is it, Nora? You can talk to me . . ." I rubbed her back in the same manner I had when she was young and couldn't sleep because our house had different sounds than her own.

She cried for some time. And when Clara peeked her head into the bedroom with wet hair and saw Nora huddled on my lap, she backed out quietly, giving us the time we needed.

"Nora? Talk to me," I pled when her tears died down.

"I've always felt like an outcast. I've always been misunderstood. Nobody has gotten me like your family does—not even my own. Clara was always my safe harbor, and I was jealous of her for having a home that I felt so comfortable in. At times, I never wanted to leave. But I love my mom. I do!" she said, conflicted.

"Shh, it's OK. You don't have to choose, Nora. You have us both."

"I just feel like I'm betraying her when I'm over here. And I feel like I can't love you without taking from her. And I know she's not my mom, but she raised me. I mean, you kind of did too . . ."

"She *is* your mom. She is!" I said.

"But, then what are you?"

"I'm . . . I'm your mom too. But you don't have to see it like that if it makes you feel torn. You can picture me as an aunt or just your sister's mother. Whatever you feel comfortable with. But I'm here for you, either way."

"I can't have two moms!" Nora huffed.

"Why not?" I asked.

"Well . . . because, nobody else does," she said, wiping her cheeks free of tears.

"Honey, I think we already know we're unlike any other family. Being unique is just a part of who you are. How many kids can say they survived death?" I asked, and Nora chuckled. "Seriously, you're so special. And you have a long road ahead of you. I don't mean to worry you, but you could use all the support you have. Let me be there for you."

"You are there for me. You always have been," Nora said, craning her neck and looking into my eyes for the first time in a long while.

"I have been and always will, but you've got to let me in."

"OK," she said, sitting up. As if it were that simple. "Do you remember my old boyfriend Landon?" she asked.

"Yes."

"There was a time when I felt like I was starting to care for him . . ."

"Yeah . . ."

"And I shut it off. Like a light switch, I just shut it off. I got scared, and I pulled back. And I told myself I'd never be as stupid as Clara. I saw what it did to her, and I saw the lackluster way Trent looked at her. I knew she would get hurt, and I knew she was allowing herself to do so. It just seemed so . . . so avoidable. I don't know why anyone would do it. I just wished that she was smarter, you know?"

I thought about what she said. She was right, in a way. Clara did get hurt, and it could have been avoided had she read the warning signs and made different decisions. But she gave herself to that boy, and her heart broke. "While Clara got hurt, I'm so proud of her for allowing herself to fall—and for trusting herself."

"You're proud of that?"

"I am. Her judgment was off"—I shrugged—"but if we can't trust ourselves, then who can we trust?"

"True . . . I hate to admit it, but I never wanted Clara to be loved back by Trent. She already had this place, she had you and Easton, and she always knew who she was. I still don't know who I am. I feel like she and I are so similar but so, so different. If that makes any sense at all. I know I'm rambling."

"I understand," I said. "But please don't be jealous of your sister. She never chose this life—none of us did. And Nora, nothing good ever comes from being closed off. Just ask Easton about that."

Nora frowned. "Ask Easton? Why?"

"Well, he could tell you better than I, but he spent many lives loveless. He too saw all the pain, and he closed himself off to the world. And if you can't grasp what really matters in life, honey, then you're going to wind up back here repeatedly, until you get it right."

"I know," she said, saddened. "What will happen to all of you?"

"Good question," I said with a small smile.

She pulled her knees up to her chin and wrapped her arms around her shins, content on the edge of my bed. "I like this. I think I want more talks like this."

"I like this too. And we can talk all the time! Day or night, you know I'll be here. Even if you just want someone to listen."

"OK. Thank you."

"You don't have to thank me," I laughed.

"Um, Mrs. Green? Do you think I could call you Mom?"

Nora's eyes glassed over, and I could see that she was nervous to put her heart on the line. It was a big step for her. Without thinking, I grabbed her and squeezed her close.

"I would love that!" I said. The tension slowly but surely drained from Nora's rigid body, and she came to embrace me the same as I did her. It was the first time I felt her love since she thought I sold her on the black market. And I couldn't have thought of a better Mother's Day gift.

"Well, I should get going. I know Clara has been waiting for me," she said.

"Patiently! Very patiently!" called Clara from the other side of the door. We all laughed, breaking the tension.

Nora rose from the bed, and just before she walked out, she turned and said, "Happy Mother's Day . . . *Mom*."

I smiled as she disappeared into the hall. My throat stung as my heart swelled, and I was left alone in the quiet house, reflecting on how far I'd come. I rubbed the tiger's eye stone hanging from my ear as I heard Brooklyn's voice ring through my head. *"You're wearing a teal scarf and these tiger's eye drop earrings that you cherish. I don't know why . . ."*

CHAPTER 20

When Clara was called on stage to receive her high school diploma, I jumped to my feet, screaming. The pamphlet was beaten and battered by the wild clapping. And when she moved her tassel from one side to the next, my heart jumped. Time stood still, and I beamed with pride. It was deep within that pride that I forgot to take a picture. "Shit! I didn't get a picture!" I said, jaw dropping. How could I be so irresponsible?

"I got it," said Brooklyn to my right. She cupped her hand over her camera, checking the picture.

"Oh, thank god!" I said, fanning myself with the battered pamphlet. The day was hot, and the lotion I had put on my legs was melting into a slick, sweaty mess. Tanner leaned forward, craning his neck to see Brooklyn as she spoke. He had recently announced his divorce, and since then, was spending extra time at our house. And if I didn't know any better, he'd been spending extra time looking at Brooklyn, too. She felt it. We all did, and it made for a very awkward graduation.

I loved Charlie; we all did. But over the years, she and Tanner grew apart instead of growing together. It had been a long time since I saw Tanner look at Charlie with love and admiration in his eyes. It was common—more common than I'd like to admit. But many of our friends had separated over the years. It seemed that "till death do us part" was rare these days. I still spoke to Charlie and would continue to do so, but it would never be the same between us. I knew she would eventually need to put distance between herself and our family to heal.

Brooklyn leaned back in her chair, out of Tanner's line of sight. She leaned into me and whispered, "Is he still looking at me?"

I didn't have to look at Tanner to know. He was still perched on his elbows, his stare blistering like the sun. "Uh-huh," I said, lips pursed.

"I think Nora is coming up," Lindsay said from the row behind us.

"Oh, OK! I gotta get a picture!" I said, fumbling with my phone.

Brooklyn placed her hand over mine. "I've got this. You just enjoy the moment." I smiled, grateful for such a thoughtful friend. I'd probably butcher the picture anyhow, and Brooklyn was a talented photographer.

"Nora Faye!" I jumped to my feet once more and hollered as loud as I could. Easton laughed, patting me on the shoulder. I reached my hand up high in the air and waved my pamphlet, hoping she would get a glimpse of us.

I couldn't be so sure, but I thought I saw her spot us in the crowd. She moved her tassel to the side of her cap and my heart fluttered once more. My cheeks hurt from smiling, and there was a possibility that I would have no voice by the next morning. I may have been more excited than the girls themselves, but that was just a part of being a mother.

Nora walked off stage, and we all took our seats once more. "Seriously? Every picture is of Becca's arm!" Lindsay said. I slumped down in my seat, afraid to turn around. Lindsay thrust her phone over my shoulder to show me the pictures of Nora receiving her diploma. Only my blurry arm was visible.

"I'm so sorry!" I said, turning around to see Lindsay. Her brows were knotted, and her jaw clenched tight.

"How's this?" Brooklyn showed her the pictures she had taken. I watched relief wash over Lindsay, and I knew that I owed Brooklyn for saving me not once but twice that graduation.

"Thank you," I said, leaning into Brooklyn.

"Any time. Is he still looking?" she asked.

This time, I needed to check, and when I did, Tanner's eyes flicked to mine. I looked away as quickly as I could and then stared straight ahead. "Yup," I said, watching the girls' friends walk across the stage.

"Is it seriously this hot outside? Or is Tanner boiling my blood right now?" she asked in a low tone.

"No, it's really this hot. I'm drenched," I said, fanning myself with the weakened pamphlet. I looked down the row at Easton and Tanner and then behind me at Lindsay and John. Everyone looked like they had just emerged from a sauna, and pamphlets were waving everywhere throughout the sea of parents.

When the ceremony was over and we found the girls in the sea of graduates, I slipped leis over their heads and tried not to cry. Brooklyn snapped several pictures of the girls together. Clara's pale blond hair against Nora's dark. They were the perfect yin and yang; complementing each other in the best possible ways. Later, I would frame one of the several pictures from that day of both the girls, and it would be one of my favorites of all time.

Since Tanner's divorce, he had been spending all of his free time at our house. The girls had moved out for college, and Tanner had practically moved in. It was fitting for all of us because neither he nor Easton and I wanted to feel alone. And in the absence of Clara, that is exactly how we felt.

Having an empty nest was an odd mix of emotions. I was beyond proud to have raised Clara so that she was mature and resilient enough to take care of herself, leaving the safety of our home to venture out into this world alone. But at the same time, I didn't want her to leave. I didn't want her to grow up. I knew I didn't have a choice, though, and I tried my hardest not to let the girls see that I was barely holding it together. When they left for college, I promised I would visit them and they made me promise . . . not too much.

So, the days settled with Easton, Tanner, and me. Much like it had been before we ever had children. I'd cook dinner for three and have extra beers in the fridge. I'd leave clean sheets in the guest bedroom and a spare toothbrush in the bathroom. And even though Tanner had been my brother-in-law, I sometimes looked after him like a child.

But when Easton and Tanner would leave for work—they'd been putting in extra hours because of a staff shortage—I stayed home and felt the effects of the empty house. There were no more little footsteps running through the home. Bodie had passed long ago, and everything remained untouched in silent stillness. I spent my time at the park, coffee shop, or on long drives that ended in the same place they started. I did anything to get out of the house—that quiet vortex that left me anxious.

One particular day, when I missed the girls deeply—and no amount of cleaning or errands seemed to help—and Easton had his first day off in a long while, he came to me with a flower picked from the side yard. The small daisy twirling between his fingers and a wicked smile reaching across his face.

"It's been really quiet in this house lately, and I know I've been spending so much time at work. Let me make it up to you. Let's go out today? We can hike and have a picnic at our spot by the Truley River? It's been years since we've been there . . ." Easton said, handing me the daisy.

I took the flower. "I'd love that," I said, bringing the flower in for a sniff. We packed a brunch—ham and cheese, croissants, and a thermos of hot coffee—and then we were on our way. Easton was in a pleasant mood, and if I didn't know any better, I'd say he was hiding something. A surprise of sorts. I tried not to let my mind wander for fear of disappointment, but it ran the gauntlet, anyway. He could have already set up a romantic picnic there early this morning. His face had seemed a little flushed when he approached me with the flower. I thought back to the daisy; had it been from our side yard like I originally thought? Or had it been a species that grew wild in the fields of the bluff?

The bluff . . . I thought little about the last time we had been there, but now that my mind was searching for answers, I let it wander. It was the first time I had been cleared since my c-section to exercise. Clara had started smiling at me for the first time. It was something I'll never forget—the moment she recognized me as the person who loved her most. And though it was a monumental event in my life, it hurt knowing that Molly should have been right alongside her . . . smiling at me for the first time, too. Every good thing that happened was laced with the bitter taste of mournfulness, and I found it hard to be happy. It seemed like ages ago.

But something happened when we went to the bluff that day to release Molly's ashes. I watched her playing in the fields behind me. A little girl chasing dragonflies. It wasn't her, of course. It had only been a figment of my imagination; but when I saw the ashes flutter through the sky, I knew it hadn't been her. I couldn't explain it then, and I still struggle to find the words now. Not that I knew she was still alive—I didn't. I only knew that she wasn't in that urn, and that was enough to carry me for many years to come.

I hadn't been back to the bluff where Easton and I

married when I was sick—the place where he proposed to me a lifetime later. I hadn't been back since we said goodbye to Molly. And I worried it would bring back the emotions of losing her, and that I'd be lost in the darkest memories of crying myself to sleep in the garage nearly every night. I was afraid to go back to a time when I thought I may actually die of a broken heart.

"You're awfully quiet," Easton said.

"I just . . . haven't had my coffee yet," I said. I took in a deep breath and looked out the window as we pulled off the side road where the head of the trial began.

"Ready?" Easton cupped my shoulder with a wide smile.

"Ready," I said.

I followed Easton when the trail grew narrow, and we walked hand in hand when it widened. We talked about the day we were there last and speculated on how it may have been different had we known then what we did now. When we were close and the trail grew narrow again, Easton stopped me, rifling through his backpack. "Wait one second."

"What are you looking for?" I asked.

"Just hold on," he said. He pulled out a red paisley bandana from his pack and rolled it.

"What are you doing?" I said in a coy tone.

"It's a surprise. The bluff is just around the bend—"

"I know that—"

"I want you to put this on. And I'll lead you," he said, holding out the bandana.

I smiled. "OK." He tied the cloth around my head and

secured it tightly in the back. I reached up, adjusting it around my eyes. "OK, I can't see a thing. Don't let me trip."

"I won't. Follow me," he said, taking my hand and leading me forward.

The trail comprised of packed dirt, and as long as I kept my feet one in front of the other, I'd stay on the trail easily enough. The grass grew taller as we rounded the bend and nipped at my shins with every step. Easton's hand was warm and clammy, and I could tell he was nervous about the sunrise. It only made me nervous about my reaction. I hoped it would be everything he wanted.

"OK, stop right there." I reached up towards the bandana. "No! Wait!" he said. I dropped my hands, listening for clues. And when there had been no sound other than the wind rustling in the trees, I pictured our picnic blanket near the cliff, a bottle of champagne and orange juice.

Easton said nothing, but I felt his proximity close in. And even though I couldn't see, I knew I had been eclipsed by his shadow. I felt his hands press against my bandana and the pressure on my eyes eased as he lifted it off my head. Easton gazed into my eyes with loving trepidation. I couldn't read what had been behind them, but when he leaned in and kissed me deeply, I imagined it was desire that I had misread as apprehension. With my eyes closed and his mouth on mine, I was taken back to the bliss we once shared in this very field. A small moan left my lips.

Easton pulled back, his hands still cupping my cheeks. And his blue eyes twinkled before he stepped out of my line of sight. I sucked in a piercing breath when I saw the surprise. It wasn't the picnic planned for two, a bottle of champagne on a rose-covered blanket, but a deserted construction site and the makings of a custom home overlooking the Truley River. My jaw dropped and hung open as I took several steps forward, unable to believe my eyes. A large tractor sat vacant off to the side. The field was dug up, exposing the rich soil. Exposed beams framed the home, as work had begun some time ago.

"I know you've been struggling with the girls moving out. And it had always been my dream to build you a home here. I was going to wait until it was complete to show you, but you've been so down lately. I just thought that maybe if you knew why I had been 'working late,' then maybe you would have a reason to shift your focus from an empty nest to the next chapter in our lives. There's a lot that needs to be done, and I was hoping you could help. I know you've been driving around aimlessly." Easton shrugged, looking back toward the home. "Now you can drive here, instead," he said.

"This . . . is ours?" I asked. Easton laughed, but it was no joke; he was serious. "This is ours?" I repeated.

"Yes! This is our new home! We're going to have coffee every morning on the porch. It's going to wrap around the entire house. We're going to open our windows at night and listen to the river run . . ."

"Can I throw flower seeds all over the field? And have a white picket fence?" I asked.

Easton laughed, "You can have whatever you want!" he said.

My chest fluttered, and I blinked several times, trying to

regain composure. I turned to Easton, the man who never ceased to amaze me. "I want you," I said with deep desire. The next bits were a blur, but before I knew it, we were making *new* memories in a place I'd one day call my kitchen.

couldn't take the chill any longer. I didn't know if it was the cancer, the raging storm outside, or the simple fact that I was frail and my body had lost its efficiency in my older age. I cranked up the thermostat several degrees and made a pot of tea. Once my bones warmed some, I sat down at my desk to finish my farewell letters. I was halfway through Nora's when I was caught in a memory and the chill set in, rendering me useless.

I tapped the pen on my lips, remembering when John had passed. We were all beside ourselves. But we found strength in each other. At least that's what I had thought. Although, Lindsay never fully recovered and she didn't wait too long before following John. I wrote to Nora about how wonderful her parents were, and how much her mother meant to me.

As I sat there—pen in hand—I reflected on my relationship with my own mother, and how we never spoke of my adoption. She passed unexpectedly, and I never took the chance when she was alive to tell her that I knew her deepest secret. That I loved her even more for raising me when she didn't have to. I knew holding that in was a great detriment to her wellbeing, but even so, I never took the opportunity to talk to her about it. Because, well, it was awkward. I shouldn't have allowed something so meaningful to get swept under the rug like that. Had my mom known that I accepted her, blood or not, it very well could have lifted a burden so heavy that it changed her life. Perhaps she would have lived longer. It was something I thought about all the time. Something I regretted. And I was so thankful that the day had come when we had the opportunity to tell Nora the truth, as difficult as it had been.

I focused my eyes back on the page and realized I was running out of room. I pressed the pen to the paper, and I wrote for Nora to love fiercely. Love like she couldn't be broken and when she fell apart, broke and shattered—and that she would—to do it all over again.

I told her to live fully. Live like fear didn't exist. Live like there's no time like the present . . . because perhaps there's not, and living with regret is no way to do it. I had learned that lesson once upon a time. And I was still learning it today.

And lastly, I told her to laugh. Life is a whole lot better with deep, gut-wrenching laughter. And if it makes her cry or even makes her wet her pants . . . that's the good stuff. I told her not to take life so seriously, and when she finds the person who makes her laugh harder than she ever had, to hold on to them tightly. They don't come around all that often.

I sipped my tea and stared out the bedroom window. The rain pelted down, turning into hail momentarily. I stopped to watch. Clicks and clacks spackled my window, and I listened to the melody of Mother Nature. I was going to miss the rain, among many other things. I swallowed, but the lump in my throat remained. I knew I had two more letters to write and that I was running out of time. I worried about where Easton had run off to and quickly dispelled the thought of him trying to leave this world first so that he could be the one to greet me with open arms. That wouldn't be very gentlemanly of him. I sighed and gripped my pen to write my dearest friend, Brooklyn, a few words to take with her after I passed.

I told her that she had been a guiding light for me all these years. That I would have been so lost without her. I thanked her for all the sacrifices she made in her own life to help the lost souls that wandered this earth long after they should have. And I asked her to take a chance on herself sometime. It didn't have to be now, or even in this lifetime, but that she should strive to find a balance between giving and receiving. While she had always been happy to give, she refused to receive anything entirely for herself. And she needed so much more than she had allowed herself to have.

Brooklyn always reminded me of the speech given on airplanes before takeoff, when they say to put your own mask on before helping others. She never abided by that rule, and sometimes I would see her struggle with little oxygen. If she only realized that she could help the other passengers more effectively if she could get a full breath;

then, I think her life would find balance. And I wanted that for her.

I asked her to look after Nora. I knew Nora would walk this earth for some time. Stuck in a vortex that she didn't yet have the strength to find her way out of. I asked that Brooklyn guide her and, when necessary, push her. I knew she would take care of my daughter long after I had gone, and I couldn't thank her enough. But it didn't stop me from trying. And by the time I finished, I had tears in my eyes.

One letter left. And it was the one I couldn't find the words for. How would I say goodbye to the love of my life? My soulmate, and yet, so much more. Easton wasn't just a husband or a lover. He had been an anchor in my life. He'd been my home.

I tried not to let the tears fall as I wrote the one thing I could. The one thing I knew how. A simple sentence. Written in cursive diagonally across the middle of the blank page. I stared at the paper and the blinding white of the empty lines. The ink blurring in and out of focus. Should I have said more? No. I didn't think so. He already knew. But this . . . this one line . . . this was a promise.

I closed my journal and wrapped it with a large burlap bow, much like the one my first mother used to wrap my childhood journals in. I left it on my desk—one last goodbye gift. Easton already knew that he needed to share the journal with all the girls. Brooklyn included. And that I'd like everyone to read it at one point or another. It was my voice that would carry on long after I passed, and that made me happy.

I stood, in pursuit of one last gift I wanted to leave with

the journals, when I heard the front door close and Easton shudder down the hallway. I walked slowly, my hand trailing the walls for support. Easton stood sopping wet in the living room, holding the most beautiful bouquet of white lilies and pink roses that I had ever seen. He closed the distance between us, leaving a trail of wet footprints on the floor. I smiled, taking the bouquet from him. I smelled the invigorating aroma of fresh flowers and I closed my eyes as the baby's breath tickled my nose.

"I just couldn't let you go without giving you flowers one last time," Easton said. My smile faded as his words sank in. His hair was plastered to his forehead, and rainwater dripped down the sides of his temples. Droplets clung to his lashes. And his eyes were red. Though he was much older now, it reminded me of the first time I looked into his eyes on that fatefully stormy night. He had been rain-soaked then, and his eyes were filled with the same heartbreak I saw in them now.

"Thank you. They're so beautiful," I said, looking out the window. I couldn't face him knowing that I had been the one that hurt him.

"What is it?" he asked.

"You know, I was just thinking of the first time we met. You were on the bridge and I had just received my diagnosis. The first time." I shrugged. "We were so young and hopeless. You just reminded me of that evening," I said.

"I did?"

I reached out, cupping his wet cheek. "You did." I dared to look into his eyes.

He turned ever so slightly, kissing the palm of my hand.

And though my final curtain was drawing near, I still got butterflies in my stomach when his lips pressed against me.

"I think . . . I think I want to feel the rain. I want to feel it one last time. And I want to remember that day that we met and our lives changed forever."

"You want to go outside? But it's cold—"

"I'm doing it!" I said, leaving. "Well, are you coming or not?" I asked, halfway to the door.

"I'm right behind you," he said. And together we stepped out of the house and stood on the edge of the covered porch. The rain was lighter than it had been that morning, and I was glad there was an opening for me to step out into the rain and not be swept away. I slipped my hand into Easton's as we stepped out into the storm. At first, it was jarring. The rain pelted down, smacking my head and slapping my cheeks. I squinted as the assault took place. I fought to open my eyes enough to see Easton. But when he stood in front of me, hands out to my side and a concerned look on his face, I felt the need to be my strongest self. I wanted to show him that I could do it and that I was still the same soul I'd always been even though my body had been failing me. "Are you OK? Let's get you inside!"

"No! I want this!" I shouted over the rumbling thunder. I held onto Easton's arm for support and slowly tilted my face up to the sky. My eyes closed as the raindrops fell onto my cheeks and dripped down my lips. I parted my mouth and caught the rain on my tongue—drinking the angel's tears. It was a marvelous feeling—the freshwater that fell from the clouds on top of my skin.

On a day that I thought I wouldn't feel anything other than the pain, I smelled the fresh roses and I drank the rain. It washed away any fears that I had lingering in the depths of my mind. And I knew that whatever force of nature was out there, that I'd soon be part of it. Maybe I'd been the one to draw in the thunderclouds? Or paint the fields with wildflowers? Maybe I'd be the girl who sent stars shooting through the sky when someone needed a wish? A smile parted my lips. I could be anything I wanted when I died. I wanted to try it all. Easton's laugh echoed and rose above the storm.

I turned to see him, and his head was tilted back, a hand crossed his chest. He was laughing harder than I'd seen in years. It reminded me of the time he saw the tattoo etched across my ribs in Sin City. And though it had faded quite a bit, I still smiled when I saw it in the mirror to this day. Easton bent forward, his laughter building still. And I watched one of the most beautiful sights I had ever seen. His unruly wet hair and flushed cheeks brought me back to a time when I was young and the days were endless. I felt that way now—that my time was infinite. And I knew that while my body was anything but, that something inside of me would go on forever.

Easton took me in his arms, wrapping one hand around my back, and holding my hand in his, and we danced. Right there in our field overlooking the Truley River—fogged in and mysterious, wet and spontaneous—we danced. Slowly, we swayed from side to side. A melody that only we could hear. Our feet never leaving the ground. I pressed my head against his chest and whispered, "I'm going to miss this." And I was glad when the storm overshadowed my voice.

I closed my eyes, my heart spilling over until the storm grew cold once more. Lightning lit the sky, and I opened my eyes just in time to see the electricity snap above the canyon and scatter into finger-like voltage. We turned slightly to watch as the blue glow lashed downward, and when the crack of thunder hit, rumbling the very ground we stood on, we knew our last dance had come to an end.

Easton ushered me inside. My teeth were chattering and my hair dripping. He ran a warm bath straight away and helped me peel the wet clothing off my frail body. "I'm so cold," I said. My voice had strained from calling out in the storm and was now no more than a hiss.

"I know, I know. This bath should help warm you up," Easton said, his hand under the faucet. I turned to see myself in the mirror and didn't recognize the woman staring back at me. Her eyes were sunken and her lips blue. Her clavicle prominent on her bony frame. Ribs covered in gooseflesh. My eyes trailed slowly down her body as I refused to believe it was mine.

Easton helped me step into the tub, and I sat down, shivering uncontrollably. He enveloped my hand in his own and blew hot air to warm my frigid fingers. I leaned forward, grasping my knees as the water rose just above my ankles.

"Don't worry, I'm going to get you war—"

"Easton?" I interrupt him. "Do you remember when Nora graduated from law school?" I asked.

He looked at me, confused. "Yeah?"

I struggled to control my breathing, which was growing ever more labored. My body was having a hard time regulating basic needs like breath and temperature. But I no longer felt the cold. "It's our granddaughter's birthday in three days . . ." I whispered.

Easton stilled, his clothes dripping on the bathroom floor. "I know . . ." he whispered back as his gaze left mine for the running bathwater.

CHAPTER 22

Smile!" Lindsay called out. I squeezed Nora's waist, and she stopped whispering to Brooklyn for a moment to smile for the camera.

"OK, now you get in here!" I said to Lindsay.

"I'll take the picture," Brooklyn said, nodding at Nora. The two of them had been talking quietly all day, and it only made me more curious. Lindsay put her arm around Nora, and the three of us beamed with pride. "Wow, that's a great one!" Brooklyn cried, examining her camera.

"Hey, what have you two been talking about all day?" I asked casually.

"Nothing," Nora said, never making eye contact. I sighed. I hated when the girls hid something from me. I spotted Clara in a blue summer dress wading through the sea of law school graduates.

"Did you find the restroom alright?" I asked.

"Yeah, it's a hike, but it's on the far side of the building if you need it," she said.

"You missed all the pictures!" Brooklyn griped. "OK, one more, guys!"

Nora threw her head back in protest as Clara joined in. The twins in the middle and the moms on the outside. "Seriously though, I can't take one more picture!" Nora said.

"You sound like your father!" Lindsay said.

I kissed Nora on the forehead. "Wow, my sweet Nora—a lawyer!" I said.

Nora rolled her eyes. She was embarrassed, but somewhere behind the annoyance, I could see a hint of a smile. "I still have to take the bar exam, Mom."

"But I thought you were a lawyer now?" Clara asked.

"I am."

"Then why do you have to take another test? You just graduated," Clara said, frowning.

"Because I'm not an attorney until I pass the bar."

"What? That doesn't make any sense." Clara's voice was sharp as she became aggravated. The sun was warm, and the crowd of graduates was a lot to take in.

"She's a lawyer now that she graduated, but she still needs to pass the bar exam. When she passes, she can then work as an attorney in that state. She's not an attorney until she can work. Did I get that right, honey?" I asked. Nora nodded, barely listening.

"So you just went through seven years of school, and you're not qualified to work?" Clara said.

"No—"

"Why isn't the bar exam just the finals then? Like why

are we even celebrating if you're not done yet?" Clara asked. She had a good point, but I knew she was trying to get under Nora's skin. Nora shot her a look that could kill.

"Clara, stop. We're celebrating because it's deserved," I said.

"Ready to get out of here?" Lindsay asked. The look in her eyes told me she had been ready to part from the crowd long ago, and she wasn't the only one.

"Yes!" Nora said.

"OK, we just have to find the men," I said, scanning through the crowd.

"They're right where we left them," Lindsay said, pointing to the graduation seating. They never came with when we moved around campus in search of backdrops for our photoshoot. If I stretched my eyes as far as they would go, I could make out a couple of tiny black suits occupying two seats in a field of white fold-up chairs. We made our way back to Easton and John as I positioned myself behind Nora and Brooklyn, trying to eavesdrop on their secret conversation.

"How much?" Nora asked.

"A lot," Brooklyn said.

"But how much? Do you know?"

"Millzsss." *Millzsss?* Millions? Were they talking about money? I hurried, stretching my neck as close to the secret as I could.

"Wow . . ."

"And that's only the first one," Brooklyn said. Nora turned enough for me to see that whatever they had been talking about had made her ecstatic. The sunlight danced atop the apple of her cheek as I caught her profile. Clara hung back to walk with Lindsay and me. And it was clear that she, too, wasn't part of the secret conversation.

"Are you OK?" I asked Clara.

"Yeah, it's just hot."

"That it is," I said, watching Nora and Brooklyn laugh. "What do you think those two are up to?" I asked.

"Nothing. Brooklyn's just handing out fortunes like she's a gypsy is all," Clara said, her tone deflated.

My stomach dropped. Brooklyn didn't speak of her dreams all that often, and when she did, it was because it was important. Monumental. Life-altering, even. I worried what she would possibly say to Nora that she hadn't said to me first. And I wondered why Nora had found so much joy in it.

"Did she tell you yours?" I asked. We were coming up on Easton and John, and it looked as though they had finally found common ground to stand upon. They, too, were deep in conversation.

"Yeah, but it wasn't anything like what she's telling Nora. She basically told me I was going to be a loser."

"What?" I highly doubted that. Although it was unlike Brooklyn to be talking about her dreams with the girls in the first place.

"Yeah, nothing even happens in my life. I just get married and have kids. It's totally predictable. Totally safe. Totally boring!" Clara crossed her arms, and the blue summer dress pinched beneath her arms.

"What!? No! Having a family isn't boring! You girls are

the best thing that ever happened to me!" I said, reaching out for her arm.

"Whatever," Clara said, accepting a life of complacency.

"What did she tell Nora?" I asked, my concern growing, as Brooklyn and Nora had been inseparable throughout the graduation ceremony.

"Oh, nothing much. Just that she's a multimillionaire, super-successful attorney who dates all these famous actors and models—"

"What?"

"While I'm here marrying Nora's high school sloppy seconds, Landon."

"But I thought you loved Landon?" I asked, watching Clara's chin begin to quiver.

"That's not the point, Mom. The point is that my life is boring. I might as well die now," Clara said, her voice barely hanging on.

"Hey! Don't say that!" I hissed. I was going to have a talk with Brooklyn as soon as we got home. Easton joined my side, taking my hand in his as we walked to the parking lot. Clara and I fell quiet, the tension thick.

"Everything OK? I'm sensing—" Easton began.

"It's fine, Dad!" Clara cut him off just before she walked ahead of us. Easton raised his brows and then turned to me for answers.

I sighed. "It seems that someone has been handing out premonitions as graduation gifts . . ." I motioned to Nora as she walked, interlocking arms with Brooklyn.

"Ahh. And Clara is jealous?" he asked.

"Well, yes. But it's only a matter of perspective."

It was late when Lindsay and John took off. Both Nora and Clara had parted immediately after dinner to spend time with their friends while the rest of us enjoyed each other's company and drinks at our house. Easton pulled out a deck of cards, intending to play poker, but the conversation never stopped long enough for him to deal. Every now and then, he would re-shuffle the deck, arch them into a bridge and tap them on the dinner table.

"Well, I should head out, too. It's late, and it's been a long day," Brooklyn said, as the door closed behind Lindsay and John and the room fell quiet.

"Actually, I wanted to talk to you about something," I said.

"Oh, boy," Easton said, leaning back into his seat. Brooklyn crossed her arms, already expecting a lecture.

"Did you tell the girls what their futures hold?" I asked, already knowing she had.

"Yes. It was a gift to Nora. But then Clara felt left out, so, I told her, too," Brooklyn said unapologetically.

"I thought we agreed that would not benefit them. That it would interfere with how their life progressed, and their efforts in doing so, that it would—"

"—Yeah! We did! But Nora has a really bright future ahead of her, and I wanted to share it! You saw how happy she was today!" Brooklyn said. It reminded me of the way some grandparents spoiled their grandchildren with cookies, candies, and cakes, only to send them home to the parents, a sugar-high terror.

"I did. But did you notice how *unhappy* Clara was?" I asked.

"I mean, she has a great future, too. It's just not as flashy as Nora's. But flashy isn't really Clara's speed, anyhow."

"Well, I know that, but she doesn't," I said.

"What do you mean by flashy?" Easton asked.

"Oh, you know, dating supermodels and rolling in cash," I barked. Brows raised and lips pursed.

"I didn't say that!" Brooklyn defended.

"That's what Clara gathered from the conversation."

"Look, I may have mentioned some men she would meet as being big names in the industry, and I may have mentioned something about the mega cases she would win . . . but what's the big deal? She's happy!" Brooklyn's mouth hung in the balance.

"I don't want her dating all these male models," Easton said, his eyes unfocused as he undoubtedly imagined something scandalous that he couldn't unsee. I frowned, just thinking about it.

The room quieted as both Brooklyn and I questioned Easton's point of view. I took a deep breath, feeling defeated. What was said was said, and there wasn't much point in arguing about it now.

"Can you promise me you will stop telling the girls about your dreams? It just doesn't feel right," I said. There wasn't much else I could say, but I knew I wanted the girls to walk their own paths, not the one Brooklyn dreamed up.

"OK. I can promise you that. For now. But when you're gone, and it's just Nora and I . . . I don't know if I can keep that promise," she said.

"Brooklyn, just try. Just try to imagine you have her best interest at heart, OK?" I asked, taking a dig.

"I do have their best interest at heart. I just don't believe it makes a difference if they know what will happen before it does. And you want to know why? Because it doesn't! I've seen it! And the picture never changes, whether or not I tell it. So, why not have a little fun where fun is needed?" she asked.

"I don't know. Obviously, I don't see what you do. It's just a protective feeling I have. It's like cheating or something," I said.

"And you don't cheat?" she asked.

"No! I don't cheat!" I snapped. Easton shuffled the cards with a smile on his face. He knew a different story. It only made me angry.

"So, you don't want to know the thing I was going to tell you about your future?" she asked.

Heat rose to the surface of my cheeks, and I knew instantaneously that I had shoved my foot in my mouth. I swallowed the lump in my throat and dared to look at Brooklyn. A slow smile spread across her face as she took in what I knew were beet red cheeks of remorse. Triumph touched the corners of her eyes. "Uh-huh," she said, a smug look on her face as she leaned back in her chair and crossed her arms.

Brooklyn had been like a sister to me. She was there through thick and thin, and when we fought, she never took it for more than what it was.

"What thing about my future?" I asked.

Brooklyn threw her head back, laughing. Easton

chuckled as his cards fell out of order and spilled onto the table, the joker face up. "Oh, but I thought you didn't think it was morally acceptable. Wasn't it you who said it was *just like cheating*?" Brooklyn teased.

"Just tell me!" I said.

"Say you're sorry—"

I sighed, looking at Easton. His brows were raised in anticipation. Clearly, I was on the opposite side of the fence. "I'm sorry that I'm weak and can't resist temptation. I want to know what my future holds," I said.

"While that wasn't a genuine apology, I'll still allow it," Brooklyn said, eager to move on to the juicy bits. She uncrossed her arms and leaned forward, the front legs of her chair hitting the hardwood floor. I leaned forward in preparation for a glimpse into my future.

"You heard that Clara marries Landon, right?" she asked, voice low and mysterious.

"She does?" Easton asked with a broad smile. We all liked Landon, even when he had dated Nora for a few short months back in high school.

"Yeah. Try to keep up," Brooklyn said to Easton, her eyes soon flicking back to mine. "So Clara and Landon have two children. Kinsley and—"

"No! Don't tell me their names!" I snapped, wanting to preserve some element of surprise.

"OK. Weird. But, on her eighteenth birthday, she gets into a terrible accident."

"Who does!?" I asked, alarm rippling through me with a shudder.

"Kinsley."

"Oh, no!" I said, cupping my mouth.

"It's OK. She'll be OK. That's what I wanted to tell you. The odds are stacked against her, and it's a very difficult time in Clara's life. I just wanted you to know that she will pull through."

"Oh my god, thank you!" I said, grateful for the knowledge. I probably would have been sick with worry, but now, at least, I'd have hope.

"I mean, you won't be there to see it, but you'll still play an instrumental part in her recovery," Brooklyn said.

Easton's gaze snapped up from his deck of cards, and the room dropped several degrees in an instant. Tiny goosebumps prickled my arms as I nodded slowly, taking in the information. I wouldn't be alive to see my granddaughter's eighteenth birthday. Clara wasn't married yet, but she and Landon were in love. I probably had twenty years left. Every passing second was one I'd never get back.

"How do you mean I'll play a part in her recovery?" I asked in haste, cutting through the grief and focusing on the information at hand. Easton sat motionless, the deck of cards still for the first time that night.

"You see, Kinsley will be in a coma for some time. Her spirit will be just beyond the veil. Not dead but not quite alive in body or mind. You'll be able to reach her there. And she'll need your guidance and encouragement to keep fighting. You two will have a special bond, and she'll look toward you for the support she needs to survive," Brooklyn said, withdrawing her hands from the table.

I should have felt devastation. Fear of the unknown.

Heartache for knowing that I only had twenty years, give or take, to live out the rest of my life. But I felt none of those things as I focused on the one piece of information that would keep me going strong in the final chapters of my life. And that was purpose. The purpose I had beyond my death.

CHAPTER 23

When Brooklyn's premonition came true, Clara married Landon at our new home on the bluffs above the Truley River. It was the push we needed to finish the last ten percent of odd jobs. I watched my firstborn marry in the same field I had. And it felt like I'd come full circle. Easton squeezed my hand tightly as they read their vows, and I knew he had the same tugging in his heart that I had.

Clara dated several characters over the years. Some were OK, and some were not. Some were right, but the timing was wrong. Landon had remained friends with both of the girls after Nora dumped him in high school and he grew fond of Clara's kind heart. She never let the potential of hurt stop her from finding the one. And one day, she realized that he had been right in front of her all along.

Landon was easy to accept into our family. He'd been hanging around long before he and Nora ever started dating. And he would be around long after. Somewhere along the way, he had become Clara's best guy friend. He felt at home when he was over, and I often caught him making lunch in our kitchen when I hadn't realized any of Clara's friends were over. She always said that he was just a friend, but I had a hunch that she was saving him for the right time.

I watched his heartbreak when she would date other guys, and I saw the same in her when he would become close to other girls. It was clear that they cared the most for each other, so we all rejoiced when they finally gave up the act and declared they were dating. I'd never forget the look Clara gave me when I said, "Wow, you're *last* first kiss . . ." but deep down, she knew it, too.

I looked to Nora, who stood confidently behind her sister as her maid of honor. Both the girls looked stunning, but only Clara was a bleeding heart. Nora had passed the bar exam three months after graduating and immediately got to work at a large firm in the city. She was on the cusp of her first big case and I could only imagine it was the one that Brooklyn had told her about. Nora had been withdrawn as she stood behind her sister. And while her heart was also made of gold, it had been misled somewhat along the way, and dollar signs reflected in her vacant stare.

When Clara kissed her groom, Easton leaned over and planted a kiss on my lips that surely rivaled that of the newlyweds. And when we took family photos welcoming our new son-in-law, he would secretly drop his hand from the small of my back and pinch my butt. There was something liberating watching your daughter marry, and I didn't know if it was the high of the celebration or the shift in responsibility from us as parents to Landon as the husband, but it made me feel like a kid again. And judging by the playful manner in which Easton and I flirted like we were teenagers, I imagined that he felt the same way.

Clara's marriage felt like our success. It felt like we were celebrating not only her beginning but our validation. Because in that moment, we had a successful launch. And though Clara's marriage was the glaringly obvious reason to celebrate that night, Nora had become successful in her own right, too. She had learned that hard work pays off, and she never backed down from hard work like she did the opportunity to let someone in. I had to remind myself that everyone has different strengths and that one day, she too would master love in the same way she had her career.

The last reason for Easton and I to celebrate was the freedom from construction that we had been living with for what seemed like an eternity. The constant table saw screaming in the background, the drywall dust that never ended, and the lack of privacy in our own home were finally things of the past. And anywhere we looked that evening, be it at Clara or Nora, or even past them and into the rose bushes, the three-tiered fountain, or the baseboards that had stolen a month of my life. . . I was so tenderly proud of it all. And I beamed all evening long.

I celebrated that night in a way I never had before. In a way, I had always wanted to but was too embarrassed. I danced. I danced with Easton, I danced alone, I danced barefoot. And when the night was still young, I earned the name. . .

"Dancing Queen," Easton said, his hands on my hips. I

threw my head back into his chest and laughed. We fit together snugly—like two pieces of a puzzle. I had always been too insecure to dance, and sometimes I even tricked myself into thinking I didn't want to in the first place. But I always wanted to. I just didn't know how. But tonight, none of that mattered. I had a reason to celebrate, and my lack of musicality wasn't reason enough for me to stop now.

"Eww, get a room!" Nora said, passing us on the dance floor as she led a tall and handsome man behind her.

I laughed, batting my hand at her when I caught the spark in Easton's eye. "What is it?" I asked.

"We do have a room . . . We have *three*," he said, his eyes pointing toward our bedroom. My lips pursed the way they sometimes did when I felt I was doing something sneaky. Easton pulled my hand, and we passed through the crowd and vanished unnoticed. We walked through the foyer, smiling at the lingering guests inside the house. Fewer guests yet, were meandering through the kitchen, and I suspected that they knew what we were up to when we passed them in a hurry, my heels clacking down the hall. I burst out laughing, but just like the dancing that took place that night, the embarrassment didn't touch me.

Easton slammed the bedroom door and backed me up against it, kissing me eagerly. I felt the smile on his lips in the bedroom shadows. "My dancing queen," he said.

"Oh, you like that?" I asked, shoving him away from me and locking the bedroom door behind me. I reached back and unzipped my dress, swaying my hips as it slid down my body and pooled at the floor. I stepped out of the dress, my heels clacking slowly with each step I took toward

Easton. And for every step I took, he took one back. A simple game of cat and mouse.

"Show me what you got," he said.

I spun, feeling the heat creep up into my cheeks as I laughed at myself. I wasn't this girl. The girl who was sexy. The one who could dance fluidly. But I was the only one that found it funny. I was the only one that thought I wasn't her.

Easton's eyes were ablaze, and as soon as I saw them, my smile faded. I rocked my hips slowly, side to side, lowering down and then back up again. I watched his eyes trail the length of my body, encouraging me to keep dancing. I strode towards him, running my hands through my perfectly pinned hair. I knew I would regret it later, but that wasn't my concern at the moment. When I reached Easton, I pushed him down on the side of the bed. I spun to face the door, and his hands reached out to greet my curves.

Sometimes I still wonder who I was that night or what had come over me. And then I simply wish I could summon it with a snap of a finger. Live as the dancing queen when the party had all but gone. Dance while I was making dinner all alone. Maybe I would even do it in my heels.

I smiled, thinking of all the opportunities I had on a regular day to be carefree and maybe even a little sexy. We made love then, in a way that was new and exciting to us. Easton collapsed against me, and the sound of the band became loud once again. "How long have we been in here?" I asked, suddenly losing track of time.

"Not long? I don't think," Easton said, reaching for his slacks and pulling them on.

I hurried to the restroom and was thankful I had glimpsed the wild beast that lived inside before hitting the dance floor. My perfect hair was distorted, slanting to one side and nearly concave on the other. "What . . . the . . ."

"Oh, wow," Easton said, looking at my hair. "You should see the back." I frowned at him before trying to finger comb the nest into order. Easton finished buttoning his shirt, tucked it in, and buckled his belt while I directed all of my efforts to fix my hair. It wasn't ever going to look the same, but when I got it to a point that looked like maybe I had just danced the curl right out, I left it. The sun had dipped behind the horizon some time ago, and I was confident that nobody would look at my hair. And if they did, they'd see a healthy marriage, and I was proud of that. Easton zipped up my dress and kissed my shoulder. His lips lingered for a moment before he pulled away and whispered, "I love you," in my ear.

"I love you, too," I said. The fire was gone in his eyes, but in its place was the warm and consistent glow of embers that he kept for only me.

Easton peeked his head out of our bedroom door. "It's clear," he said, opening the door wide. I threw my shoulders back and strode down the hallway. As luck would have it, nobody was lingering inside the house, and nobody had witnessed our bedroom exit. At first, I was grateful, but then I wondered, *why*? I squeezed Easton's hand as soon as it hit me.

"The cake!" we said. We took off running across the kitchen and down the foyer.

When we snuck into the crowd, almost unnoticed, I could see Clara with a dot of frosting on her nose. Landon had cake up the side of his face and pressed into his ear. I smiled, placing my hand over my heart, and mumbled, "Good boy," to no one other than myself.

The guests dispersed, some to the dance floor and some to their chairs. But Easton and I stood still as we watched Clara and her new husband make a memory that would last a lifetime. I rested my head on Easton's shoulder as I spotted Brooklyn across the room. She had been watching Clara with the same pride in her eyes that we had. I thought about how she would remember this moment for far longer than the one lifetime. And how the memory would live as long as she graced this earth.

Brooklyn's head whipped around as Tanner slipped his hand in hers. She looked pleasantly surprised. I watched as a quick exchange ensued, and then he pulled her onto the dance floor. Brooklyn put her head on his chest, and he slid his hands down the small of her back. They rocked slowly from side to side, and I marveled at just how perfect they were. How perfect they had always been when they were together. I loved Charlie. She'd found a special place in my heart, but at some point in time, she and Tanner found they were better people when they were apart. It wasn't like that with Brooklyn, though. They always brought out the best in each other.

"Do you want to dance? Or are you all tuckered out?" Easton asked.

I smiled and wrapped my arms around his neck. "Never," I said.

He held me close as we slow danced. My head pressed against Easton, I searched the crowd for the bride. She was wiping down Landon's cheek with a napkin. He turned to her talking before leaning forward and licking the frosting off her nose. I giggled. They were well on their way to a happy marriage. I searched for Nora. I found her wrapped in the arms of the handsome stranger that I'd seen her with earlier. She danced with her eyes closed and a small smile on her lips. And just for that single moment under the stars that evening, everything had been perfect.

CHAPTER 24

The phone rang in the dead of the night. Alarmed and disoriented, I reached for my cell phone. Easton rolled over as I fumbled to answer it. "H—Hello?"

"Are you ready to be a grandma?" Landon asked on the other line.

"It's time? It's time! Easton, it's time!" I slapped the bed.

"We just got admitted to the hospital. Clara has hours ahead of her, but you're welcome anytime. We're on the third floor," he said.

"We're coming! We're on our way!" I shouted.

"Christ, Beck, he's having a baby, not going deaf! He can hear you!"

"Shut up and put your pants on! We've got a baby to catch!" I ran in circles frantically.

Landon laughed on the other end, and I could hear him faintly say, "Your parents crack me up . . ." Clara moaned.

"OK, we're coming! See you soon!" I said, bumping into Easton in the dark.

When the lights switched on, I was wearing a sheer lace cami and a pair of sexy boy shorts. It was a habit I started when Clara moved out of the house because why not? I didn't expect it to last longer than a week, but there I was, completely unacceptable outside of our bedroom. I looked at Easton, who was fully dressed in an impossible amount of time. I couldn't wrap my mind around it. It was mere seconds since the phone had rung.

"What just happened?" I asked.

"Do you remember when I said you would cave under the pressure? And you had the audacity to take that bet?" he said with a smug smirk.

I said nothing but rolled my eyes, in search of clothing.

"Remember when you upped the ante by saying that I would never get ready as fast as you when the call came in?"

"No! That's not what I said!"

Easton laughed.

"That's not what I said . . ."

"Then, what did you say?"

"I said . . . that I would make it to the door first," I said. And as soon as it came out of my mouth, we were racing to the front door. All in the name of diaper duty. I reached my hand for Easton, who was ahead of me by several feet as we ran through the dark house. I dug my nails into the back of his shirt, trying to grasp a handful. Anything I could use to pull him backward and propel myself forward. But it didn't happen like that.

"Door!" Easton called out as he hit the door. I slapped his shoulder and then thrust my hand on my hip. "What?

Were you ready to go to the hospital, in that?" Easton's eyes trailed down my silk and lace silhouette.

"No . . ."

He laughed again. "Then why did you even race me? Just admit that I won the bet!" he said.

"I—I raced you out of pure instinct, first of all," I admitted. Easton threw his head back, laughing, and a small smile tugged the corners of my lips out of embarrassment. "And second of all," my eyes trailed down Easton's shirt, jeans, and shoes. "Did you sleep in that?" I asked.

Easton leaned in, and though the house was empty, he whispered. "I had secret intel."

I growled ferociously. Easton was impossible to beat at a bet. I had made it my lifelong goal to win just once. But every time I lost, I only wanted it more. I spun on my heels and stomped down the hall, defeated, when Easton reached forward and slapped my butt. The thin fabric of the shorts, like a second skin, did little to protect against the sting. I paused and took a deep breath as he chuckled in triumph. Then, I continued on my way.

"Come on, Beck. We've got a baby to catch!" Easton called out down the hall.

On the way to the hospital, I couldn't help but be reminded of the time that my first niece, Everly, nearly took my life when she rounded the corner into the parking lot. I couldn't believe that we were here again. And I couldn't be more grateful that it wasn't *me* who was having another baby . . . in another lifetime.

I felt the nerves and the thrill wind up in my chest as we

waited outside of Clara's delivery room, but most of all, I was excited. I'd never been a grandparent before, and neither had Easton. I imagined it was all the best things about having kids, with none of the work. I vowed to myself that I would help Clara as much as I could . . . As much as she would let me. And even though I lost the bet to Easton, I didn't mind changing dirty diapers.

"Push!" the doctor said. I looked up at Easton, his shoulder leaning against the wall.

"OK, now breathe. Breathe. Good."

We listened through the partially opened door. I chewed on my lip, and my heart pounded in my chest as the seconds ticked by in slow motion.

"OK, now push! Push!"

Easton and I locked eyes again, waiting. We held our breath, listening.

"Good, you're doing great. Breathe." I breathed laboriously. I wasn't in labor, but I was right there alongside Clara, going through the motions. I wished I could hold her hand, so I held Easton's instead.

We breathed together. Long deep breaths in and out. And though she couldn't see us on the other side of the wall, we were there, cheering her on. I reached my clammy hands out to Easton's, and he pulled me close for support. "It's going to be OK," he whispered. I nodded against his chest.

"Now push! Push!" the doctor instructed. I pulled from Easton's embrace and sought comfort in his light blue eyes. Goosebumps pricked my forearms as I heard the first tiny, tiny cry of my grandchild.

The emotion swept over me, and tears spilled down my cheeks. I bowed my head into Easton's chest, and he rubbed my back as I wept happy tears. I knew on the other side of that wall that Clara had her eyes on her firstborn for the first time. For the first time, she had a face for all the love she'd carried for nine months. She was a mother now, and I knew just how remarkable that felt. And then . . . and then, I was taken back to a time when the miraculous feeling had slipped right through my hands, and everything had become darkly devastating. My world upside down.

I knew it would be alright because Brooklyn had told us so. But I still couldn't help but remember losing Molly, and a small part of me worried it could happen to Clara, too. But it was just fear. Fear of my own tragedy projecting onto her. And I cried it all away. Clara's baby was healthy, and it wouldn't be a Tethered Soul, either.

The doctor walked out of the room and saw us embracing outside of the door. "Ah! You must be Mom and Dad?" he asked.

"Yes," Easton said. I wiped my tears and attempted to gather myself.

"Congratulations, Mom and baby are healthy. You can go in now," he said with a pat on Easton's back.

I leaned toward the open door and called out, "Honey?" in a broken voice.

Landon popped his head out, startling me. "You want to meet your granddaughter?" he asked.

"Granddaughter?" I said, placing a hand over my heart. Pigtails and pink frilly dresses danced before my eyes. I had an entire box filled with Clara's favorites from when she was a child that I had been holding onto just in case.

"Yeah, come on in," Landon said while opening the door. Easton cupped him on the back, congratulating him as a father while I headed straight for the baby. She was a beauty. Puckered, blush, wet lips, short blond strands, and a wrinkled little face. My tears dropped on Clara's bed as I leaned over to admire my granddaughter. Clara chuckled and wiped away her own tears.

"She's beautiful, Clara," I said. Easton came up behind me, gasping in awe, as we marveled at the tiny human that captured our hearts.

"Do you want to hold her?" Clara asked.

"Me?" I smiled. I couldn't think of anything better. Clara lifted the bundle, and I took her in my arms carefully. Her face flexed in and out of a wrinkled frown, and her lips bowed and parted. I patted her back as I swayed slowly back and forth.

Holding my grandchild differed from holding my own. I wasn't sure if it was the confidence I found in the experience of raising Clara or that this was a completely different delivery than I had, but when I held my granddaughter it was like all the worry had been stripped clean, and only a fresh start remained. It was peaceful.

"Do you have a name picked out?" Easton asked.

Clara looked to Landon and smiled. "Kinsley," she said.

"She looks like a Kinsley," Easton said, and I could hear the smile in his voice. I smiled too, remembering that one day, not too long ago, it was Brooklyn who dreamed this very moment. Her voice rang in my ears *"Kinsley and—"*

But I didn't know it would feel this magical to hold her, and I was beyond myself that, one day, there would be another.

But then something else surfaced in my memory. True to form, the yin and yang of contrary forces were coming together. Always together. It was something that crowded out the light, chasing it to the outskirts of my mind and leaving darkness in its place.

My smile faded when I remembered what else Brooklyn had seen in the realm of her dreams that night. It was an accident—the severity of which I couldn't yet know. However, I knew two things. The first was that Kinsley would overcome her accident and make a full recovery one day with the help of her friends and family, and maybe even me. That piece of information did a lot in terms of reassurance, and I was thankful Brooklyn had told me, even though I gave her a hard time for spilling the future.

The second thing that rang true and that I couldn't shake—I was just shy of eighteen years away from my death date. Eighteen years seemed like a long time until you realize there was no more time after it.

"Mom?" Clara asked.

"Huh?" I looked down at Clara, and then across from her at the nurse. They were waiting for something. I hadn't even seen her come in.

"I need to feed Kinsley," she said, her hands outreached.

"Oh! Right!" I leaned over the bed, passing sweet Kinsley back to Clara.

"She's so in love, I don't think she even heard you," Easton said, his hand wrapped around my shoulder.

I smiled. "We're going to get some coffee. Just let us

know if we can get you anything," I said. Landon walked us to the door and we parted ways. We hung around the hospital for a couple more hours before giving the new family time to be alone. It was hard for us to do, but we knew it was what Clara and her family needed to bond.

When we left the hospital, I had Easton take me to the local bookstore. I browsed for nearly two hours. The smell of the books was oddly calming, and I ran my hand across the spines until one called to me. By the time Easton had pulled me from my escape, not only one book had spoken to me but many. I walked out of the bookstore, balancing a stack of books.

One for Clara on what she could expect as a new mother. A few for me to fill the nights when Easton worked late and I couldn't sleep. A psychological thriller, a mystery, and a romance. And several fairytales for Kinsley. Little Red Riding Hood, Beauty and the Beast, Rapunzel, and a couple of other classics sure to capture her heart and fill her head with imagination.

The next several months were some of my favorites. I would spend my time rocking baby Kinsley. And even though Easton handed Kinsley to me every time she soiled herself, I always took her proudly. And then I wouldn't give her back. In the evenings when Landon came home from work and Easton was heading out for a night shift, I would busy myself with babyproofing the house. Every now and then, I would get a glass of wine and talk to Nora on the phone.

Nora ended up winning her first big case like Brooklyn had said she would. But because she had known about it since law school graduation, she had a lot of time to think about how she wanted to spend the money. By the time it hit her account, most of it had either been spent or was already spoken for in various investments. And after the first big case was won, another followed. Then another. Eventually, Nora had made quite a name for herself and opened her own law firm.

She and Easton had long talks late at night about the things she could do to squander away a stash of money for her next life. And one time, he took her on a special father-daughter trip to meet some special people that would help hide her assets for her next life.

It didn't take long before Nora started dating men I had seen on the cover of a magazine or playing small roles on the big screen. They all dazzled her. Entertained her for sure. But none of them captured her heart. And during the family dinners that she brought them to, I'd always watch Easton's eyes to see if they rose above her head. I knew I had never seen her love glow for anyone other than family, but my vision wasn't as strong as hers or Easton's, and there were never wandering eyes as far as I could tell.

Some nights, I would try to pick the reason why her boyfriends weren't the ones for her, and some nights, I'd give up and throw my hands in the air. I'd blame it on Nora for not opening her heart up. But ultimately, I knew she was waiting on someone special in the way that Easton had. The very specific soul that would capture her heart, whether or not she was ready for it. And the truth was, that soul could be lifetimes away.

CHAPTER 25

The heater kicked on, and the low sound of its hum shed little hope of warming my bones. Even though I had soaked in a hot bath and Easton had dried my hair, it didn't change the fact that I was dying today. My body was frail, fatigued, and beyond the point of repair. Chills racked my body, ripping through my knobby spine. And when Easton gave me hot tea to sip, I spilled it down the front of my bathrobe in one swift convulsion.

Outside, the storm was relentless, and inside it was no different. It reminded me of the doom that once painted the sky and made its way into my heart—the day of my first diagnosis, and the day I'd met Easton. I remembered how powerful the storm was that night. And the moment I stepped out of my truck—my shoes soaked through, immediately drenched, afraid, and all but ready to give up. Just like Easton was that night.

But if I had only known what I do now, maybe I would

have spread my arms and drunk the rain. Maybe I would have looked into Easton's eyes and smiled instead of judging him for where he was in his life at that very moment. Maybe I could have made him laugh. Or maybe I would have asked him to dance in the middle of the wild storm like he and I did today.

Tiny Tommy curled up next to me on the bed, and I pet him mindlessly. He was a gift from the girls when they found out my cancer had returned. They recalled a time when I told them of my first mother and how much joy a therapy dog brought her. They remembered sweet Bodie and how loved he had been by everyone who met him. And they wanted to gift me the same support my mother once had. But Tiny Tommy wasn't a therapy dog, and I wasn't a patient who received weekly visits. The little grey dog quickly became Easton's out of necessity, because I was too tired to take care of him. But at rare times like this, when he was calm and cuddly, I found it soothing to run my hand around his ears and down his back, twisting and tangling my fingers in his long, silky hair.

"I have them," Easton said, entering the room with my two engagement rings—one old, one new. One Beck's, one Becca's.

"Can you bring the journal that's on my vanity?" I asked, pointing a knobby, quivering finger.

Easton brought me the journal and set it on my lap. I unraveled the bow and then plucked one ring from the palm of his hand and slipped it over the burlap tie. Then, I did the same with the other ring. Simple, yet challenging with dwindling motor skills. "I want Clara to have the new ring. She's made such a wonderful life for herself," I said, re-tying the bow to secure the journal. The two diamond rings dangled below the burlap.

"I want Nora to get the old ring. The one we stole from my parent's house. She will need the reminder one day that her path, while less traveled, is one that we've taken before. And that there is love on that path if she's patient."

I lifted the journal, and Easton took it gently from my hands. "There's a note for you in there. You can read that when you're good and ready," I said. Easton paused momentarily before placing the journal down on our dresser next to the bouquet he'd given me that morning. I noticed his head drop ever so slightly, and I wanted nothing more than to make him feel OK. "Easton?" I asked, my voice raw from yelling in the rain and the tumor that pressed against my vocal cords.

"Yes?" He turned around and joined me on the side of the bed.

"I don't want you to be sad," I said.

"I know you don't." He reached out for my hand, and the heat of his body felt nice against my skin.

"I'm not scared. You asked me one time if I was scared to die. Do you remember that?" Easton nodded, slowly. "I was then. But I'm not now. I feel ready. I don't want to leave you, but my body no longer works in the way I'd like it to, and it's holding me back. It hurts, and it's heavy to carry. I'm looking forward to being set free. I'm ready. I'm *ready*." I nodded.

Easton's back hunched, and he could no longer keep himself together.

"Did you hear me? I'm ready!" I said, stressing that my life wasn't being taken from me—that I wasn't a victim, but that I had earned my way out.

"You have given me such a beautiful life, Easton," I said, even though I feared he could no longer hear my whispers. I lay down on the bed and curled up on my side.

"No." He shuddered and curled up behind me, wrapping his brawny arms around my bony waist. And even though I weighed next to nothing, my body felt incredibly heavy, like it might sink into the bed and fall straight through to the other side.

The sky had been dark and stormy for days, and I had no way of knowing what time it was. But that didn't matter any longer because it was *my time*. "Tell me a story?" I asked. Though I didn't want a story and I didn't need the distraction, he did. And I wanted to hear the sweet sound of his voice, the melody of language, his unique intonation.

"A story? Um, I can do that." Easton cleared his throat and took a moment to collect himself. "Once upon a time, there was a boy—"

"Was he handsome?" I asked.

"He was *so* handsome. He was the most handsome of all the boys!" Easton said. I wanted to laugh. It felt like I had. Only, there was no sound and there was no movement.

"This boy. Despite being ruggedly good-looking, was down and out. His life was an endless loop of unfulfillment. And one day, he sought to end it. But just as he was about to take what he had thought was his only option out, he saw another path. That path was a difficult one too, as he knew it would inevitably hurt his heart more than ever before. But she was the fairest in all the land, and she had a light within her that he couldn't resist. A light so profound that he could never look back."

I imagined that night and the first time I looked into his eyes as I listened to the honeyed rhythm of his voice. His subtle inflections lulling me to sleep.

"Her light was so special that she kept it guarded—safe from the others. And sometimes, she did that so well that she forgot it was there at all. But he saw it, even when she did not." Easton tightened his grip around me and I grew even heavier.

"The boy opened his heart to the girl, and eventually, she did the same. They didn't know it then, but they had been each other's missing puzzle pieces, and once found, their masterpiece was complete. The girl couldn't understand why the boy was sad. She had been happy that their work was done. But the boy explained to her in only the way that he could. He said he enjoyed putting the puzzle together so much that he didn't want it to end."

My breathing slowed as my body continued to sink into the bed. And ever so slightly, I felt a release. A part of me was lifting, while the part that no longer served me sank. My memories, thoughts, and all of the love rose above the brittle body that was once Becca Green. And my breath fell to trivial, undetectable levels.

"But she looked at that boy . . . that ruggedly handsome boy, and she said, 'Dear, I know you enjoyed making this masterpiece with me. I enjoyed it more than you will ever know. But the best part of making art is stepping away from a finished piece and marveling at your creation.' "

I listened to the story as it rang true in my heart of hearts. My life with Easton was a masterpiece, and I wouldn't have it any other way. I looked down at Easton's arm wrapped tightly around my waist, but I no longer felt it.

"She said, 'Dear, won't you let me step away, so that I may marvel over our masterpiece?' And though he didn't want her to go, he couldn't keep her any longer. He released her, and she took several steps back. Far too many in his opinion, but the further away she got, the bigger her smile beamed. Until one day, she got so far and her pride shined so brightly that she became the sun."

I tried to lift my hand to his arm, but I could no longer move. I tried to speak, but nothing translated. I pulled back and was suddenly standing beside the bed, looking down on myself wrapped in Easton's arms. I wasn't sure if or when I had passed, as it felt like the smooth transition of falling asleep after a long day of work. I felt incredibly light, though, like I was everywhere and nowhere at the same time. But all I wanted was to be here, now. I wanted to hear the end of the story.

"And it was her sunlight that shone down on the boy every day that warmed his heart. And he, too, began to step back and see the puzzle as a masterpiece in its completion," he said. Easton paused for a moment before his head jerked upward. Swiftly, his arm that held onto my waist was on the fleeting pulse of my neck. "Beck? Beck? Just stay. Stay a little longer. Don't go. Don't go, honey," he cried.

Easton's frantic tone slowed into a vibration I could feel stirring within me. His woodsy scent came alive, dancing around me like a phantom in the night. I looked down at my hands, which were no longer trembling. The chill I couldn't shake shifted into something new—something tantalizing . . . like pleasure prickling down the nape of my neck to the small of my back. I let out my last shallow breath of air and watched and waited for the inhalation that would never come.

And then it happened. The faint beat of my heart ceased to exist, and Easton collapsed over my body, weeping in a blur of slow motion. There was a shift in my axis. The buoyancy I felt before paled in comparison. I was larger than life itself as I became a part of all the things—seen and unseen. I was limitless. Lawless. I was no longer bound by the laws of physics, suppressed by the human mind, or confined to the body that had jailed me for all the years and lives. I was untethered.

I watched Easton's back rise and fall over my body. His cried like a sad piano symphony that I could feel in my heart and hear all around me. I reached out to touch it as it whirled by, and my hand slipped inside. I pulled it back, examining my fingers. It wasn't like the first time I died, when I saw the events of loved ones before the blackness swallowed me whole, but perhaps that was because my heart was here with Easton. And I wouldn't be returning to another life on Earth.

It was nice to pass with no major regrets. I felt I had done a good job this time. I had balance. Love and happiness. I raised two of the best people I knew. It was an odd thing to look back at your lives and see them in their completed form. I had been so used to seeing it in motion.

Seeing life as it unraveled before me. But now it was fixed, only a memory. A memory that Easton was still stuck in. I didn't know why I departed earlier than he or why he couldn't have come with me, but I knew one thing . . . I would wait for him.

CHAPTER 26

"Take me with you," Easton cried as he hunched over me. What used to be me. I watched from the corner of the room, unable to interfere. It wasn't what I wanted to see, and it hurt me to be there witnessing his cutting pain. I felt it in ways I'd never felt anything before. Bold colors painted the room. A bitter taste filled my mouth and drumming coursed through my veins—energy where blood had once been. But I couldn't leave him. My heart belonged to Easton, and his to me. And when I said forever, I meant it. I would be Easton's personal angel for as many lives as he needed to live before he came home to me.

Easton cried until he nearly turned grey. I once would have worried that he would die right then and there, but now I knew. I knew he had a long life ahead of him. His work wasn't done yet; his body wasn't weak. And it was hard for him now, but he would one day look back at me with a smile. I'd do everything within my power to urge that day to come sooner than later, but for now, I'd have to ride out the storm with him. And it was the worst storm we'd seen in a long time.

"Beck . . ." Easton called out. I wanted to comfort him —show him that I was there and he need not worry. I tried. I reached out, but my efforts went unnoticed. I was invisible. Inaudible. Untouchable. I was only a memory. But I wasn't just a memory to me; I was here! I was alive! I was thriving like never before! I begged him to notice me. I grabbed his arm, firmer yet, but my grasp turned empty every time. I tried to knock over a lamp on the bedside table, but I passed straight through it. I tried to take my love and wrap it into a ball and push it toward him with all the energy I had conjured. Nothing worked. He cried all night long.

It was difficult to watch Easton cling to me. I wanted to tell him it wasn't me. I wasn't me! But he couldn't hear all the things I had to say. I watched as Easton's eyes grew heavy and my remains turned cold. The hours passed by, slow and painful. And though time didn't have the same meaning to me any longer, I knew this had to be the longest night in history. Easton's eyes fixed to nothing in particular as his heart rate slowed and the fight inside of him simmered down. It had been a good fight, but not a battle he could have won.

His eyes began to blink for longer, more restful moments. And when sleep finally took him, I came in close and whispered, "I'm here," in his ear. I watched for a sign that he heard me, but there was nothing except his twitching eyelids to tell me if my voice had reached him. I stayed there for some time, making sure he drifted off to sleep. And when I was sure that he had, I moved to the window to watch the storm lighten.

It was all but a mist when the sky lightened. The windowpane was fogging before me, even though I had no breath to share. I tried to draw a heart in the fog, but my finger passed through it. Part of me was inside the bedroom with Easton, and part of me was outside in the crisp morning air. I felt neither of them. Because I wasn't just in these two places at the same time, but I was everywhere all the time. I felt the beating heart of Clara, slow and steady. I saw my passing replayed in Brooklyn's nightmare. I felt Easton's emotions quiver like a fish on the line. I knew the rain had a distinct smell, but I no longer smelled it. I knew the early morning air was cold, but I didn't feel it.

I passed through the window with great ease. I felt no physical touch. But emotion—that was a different story. I felt everything near and far. I felt every living soul all at once, and I knew which of them were my loved ones. I dimmed the emotional potency of all others. I don't know how I did it. Instinct, I guess.

My soul buzzed with the vitals of the select handful of souls I wanted to watch over. Easton, of course. Clara and Nora. Clara's husband, Landon, and my granddaughter, Kinsley. I'd watch over Brooklyn and Tanner, too.

The moment I thought of Lindsay and my parents—the moment I thought of all the loved ones that had passed before me—a warm energy glowed in the distance. I stared at the burning light, entranced by its beauty. I knew, without a shadow of a doubt that if I wanted to, I could leave this place. This grey sky. This grief-stricken heart.

I knew I had that choice, but inside that home that Easton and I built and inside that bedroom, lay a heart that beat for me—a heart that I belonged to. And though I knew it was my time to pass on, I chose to wait instead. After all, I had been a Tethered Soul. Because I wouldn't leave Easton if it meant living an eternity unseen and unheard.

As soon as I looked away from the gleaming light, the sky grew dark in its absence. I knew I'd be here and it would be waiting. I watched the sunrise, and I felt the living rise with it. Easton's sleep lightened when Tiny Tommy jumped off the bed, and I came back inside to be there for him when he woke, not from a nightmare but to his new reality. It was harder than I imagined. I stayed close, trying to plant memories in Easton's mind. Good memories of times we had shared. He cried despite them.

By mid-morning, my body had been collected by the coroner. Brooklyn had shown up before Easton called the girls, and she did what she could to support him. It was more than I could do.

"I know it hurts, but she's in a better place," Brooklyn said.

"How do you know? How?" he asked, eyes swollen. "Did you have a dream?"

A dream? I wondered if I could penetrate Brooklyn's dreams and patch a message through to Easton. It was worth a try. I had the time anyhow.

"I did," Brooklyn said. And I knew this was the side of Brooklyn that used her insight for good—because she didn't have a dream about me—but she had the power to help ease Easton's pain. And she knew that.

"I don't know, Brooklyn. I don't know that I can live without her," Easton said.

"You've done it for so long. You can do it again."

"But that was before I knew her. Everything has changed now. Everything," he said.

"I know." Brooklyn peered out the window. "Hey, there's a rainbow!" she said, standing. Easton and Brooklyn hurried outside and stood under the most brilliant rainbow, which stretched across the sky and sank into the field. Our field. I marveled as the rainbow's end lit the long blades of grass and wildflowers. Easton's trembling hand cupped his mouth, and Brooklyn wiped away the silent tears that spilled onto her cheeks. And I stood with them, resting my head on Easton's shoulder as I took in the colors of light that spilled onto the damp field.

"The storm is finally over," Brooklyn said.

But nothing was over. Just different. I opened my senses for all things living. I sifted through the quivering lines until I found one so delicate and so hopeful that I reached out for it, sending a long breath of wind for it to ride all the way to us. When it showed, its teal wings flickered under the light of the rainbow.

Easton hadn't felt me when I grabbed for his arm, and he didn't hear me when I spoke soft words of encouragement to him as he drifted off to sleep. But he recognized my presence when I sent him the dragonfly. His jaw clenched tightly as he ran a hand through his hair. He nodded. Said nothing but he didn't have to.

We watched the rainbow until it faded away and the time had come for Easton to make two very difficult phone calls. Brooklyn asked Easton if he wanted her to stay, but he asked her to tell Tanner instead. One less phone call for Easton to make. She agreed and left shortly thereafter. Easton sat by the phone for a long time before picking it up. I wasn't privy to his thoughts, but I didn't need to be to know he was planning on what to say. I tried to give him the words. I whispered them in his ear. And I held him while he broke the news.

When it was time for Clara to break, I left Easton to be by her side. She had the support of her loving husband and her two kids, and I was thankful she took it better than Easton had. I tried to comfort the family, but I knew they'd be going through a rough patch. If they broke today, I knew they would shatter in two days' time. Kinsley was about to turn eighteen, and she'd be fighting for her life as she transitioned into adulthood. It would be the darkest time in Clara's life, but it would make her so much stronger.

Kinsley took the news harder than I expected. She and I had a special bond, and I was the first real loss that she experienced. She couldn't understand how I was there one day and gone the next. She questioned life's purpose. And I did, too. But I encouraged her to stay strong and support her mom. I watched as Clara and Kinsley talked on the sofa for hours about love and life. I listened to her theories and basked in the sporadic laughter. And though it was my passing that gave them the opportunity to bond, I was so grateful that Clara would have this moment to fall back on when she had no hope left.

Nora turned inward. She sat alone in her loft high above the city and drank wine while she watched the world below pass by. She took one day off work—which was more than I had known her to do before—and she eased her pain with alcohol. She didn't shed a tear that day, though I knew they would come in time. I thought about how difficult it was to watch Easton mourn, and then how much more difficult it was to see Nora resist it. I watched as she placed brick over brick, securing her walls. Making them stronger and even less penetrable—obscuring the signs of pain. But Nora didn't need thicker walls; she needed to remove them. Bust through them and completely crumble. Like a phoenix, she needed to burn so she could resurrect.

I reached out for her, but like Easton, I couldn't get through. However, there was a difference when I tried to comfort Nora. There wasn't a need. She didn't want my comfort. She only wanted to skirt around any authentic emotion. She wanted to bury her heart and busy her mind. And when she could no longer focus on distractions, she would numb herself in other ways. If I was invisible to Easton, it was like I had never existed to Nora. Her hurt ran deep and twisted. Branching out in unconventional paths. If there was one thing that hurt more than grief, it was knowing that you couldn't feel it at all. I knew that I couldn't help her. Time and only time would be her antidote.

I closed my eyes to Nora in her loft above the city and found myself home with Easton. He sat on the sofa, his feet up on the coffee table, warmed by the wood-burning fire and Tiny Tommy by his side. The flames flickered in his eyes, and his face wilted with defeat. On the coffee table lay my journal. The burlap bow untied, and the page open to Easton's letter.

Find me.

It wasn't a goodbye letter like the others had been. It was a challenge. If there was anything that Easton excelled at, it was a challenge. Like he had the first time our lives parted, I knew Easton would find me one day. And until then, I'd be here before his very eyes. I curled up in his lap the way I used to, and I settled in for another long night.

CHAPTER 27

 hadn't been dead for more than three days when Kinsley had her accident. I didn't need a phone call to know, and I certainly didn't need a ride to the hospital. I had been preparing for this moment for the last twenty years of my life. It was the very reason I hadn't feared dying. I knew that there was something left I had to do, and I was the only soul for the job. It brought me wells of comfort to know that I was still needed. I didn't know how I could help Kinsley during this difficult time, but I knew I could figure it out along the way. After all, everything else had come so naturally for me on the other side.

The moment it happened, I felt Kinsley's senses shift like a sharp edge. And when she fell unconscious, her emotions slipped into a void that I could no longer reach. I rode with her in the ambulance. I held her hand as the paramedics attended to her. I checked in with Clara and Landon, but the news hadn't reached them yet.

Brooklyn had only told Easton and me about the accident. And even though she spoke of it only once, and so long ago, Easton and I talked about it often—and thought about it even more. It was a marker in time that signified the end of my life. At least, the end of the predictable part.

When Kinsley reached the hospital, the pain came back tenfold, and she stirred, though her eyes remained close. The doctors rushed all about, passing through me while I stood still. I didn't know what I was looking for, but I knew I was close to finding out.

"Help me! Help!" Kinsley screamed. For a moment I stared at her face as she writhed in pain. Her body thrashed against the pillow as the doctors pushed medications. "Help me!" she screamed. I looked around me and then rose above to look down. Kinsley's calls weren't emanating from her body. In fact, they weren't from this dimension at all.

I closed my eyes and instinctively—like I'd done it a million times before—I pushed backward into the next dimension. There were many of these layers, like an onion, they'd say. And I had time to explore them all, but I wanted to do so with Easton. And until now, I'd never had a reason to leave Easton's world.

The realm was still except for Kinsley as she frantically ran about calling for help. I approached her with caution. "Kinsley? Can you see me, dear?"

Kinsley's eyes stilled, and I thought she had been looking at me, but I wasn't sure. She gasped for air, looking me up and down. I turned my attention inward. I looked almost real. Like I had when I was alive. "Kinsley?" I asked.

"Gran? Is that you?" she asked, panting. Her cheeks were flushed and pupils dilated.

"Oh, Kins—"

"—You're dead! But you're dead!" She looked down at her own body, and the fear that settled when she laid her eyes back on me now tripled.

"No! No!" I shook my head.

"Yes! You died! Three days ago! You died!"

"I . . . I—"

"Am I?" she asked.

"No!"

"Gran, am I dead?!" Kinsley cried out hysterically.

"Baby, no! You're not dead! Listen to me!" I grabbed ahold of her and was shocked when I made contact with her skin. I pulled her in close, wrapping my arms around her and stroking her hair. It felt incredible to hold her again. "That's why I'm here. I need to tell you that you're going to be OK. It's all going to be OK," I said.

Kinsley cried against my shoulder, and I could swear that the tears were real. "Gran, I'm scared!" she said, her voice splintered with fear.

"I know you are. But I'm here. I'm right here with you." A loud sound crashed down like thunder, and Kinsley jumped. "What was that!?" she shrieked.

I looked around, but there was nothing. The whole place was like a void. A waiting room for those who were split between two realms. And if I hadn't known any better, I would have guessed that we were in a cloud. Not a puffy white cloud that resembled a cotton ball but a dark grey one, misty and thunderous. I didn't feel it, but the dimension appeared cold and damp. Kinsley's arms were prickled with goosebumps, and while I worried that she could still feel the discomfort, I was relieved because it meant that she was still alive. "I don't know," I said.

"Gran, I don't want to die," Kinsley said in a hurried voice. She pawed at me frantically.

"No, it's not your time, dear. You *will* get through this. I promise."

"What's that?!" She raised her arms, searching the length of her sides for answers. I saw nothing.

"What's what, dear?" I asked.

"What's happening?" Kinsley became even more panicked, spinning in circles like a dog after its tail. I reached out for her arm to steady her, but this time . . . this time, my hand went through her and tiny shards of her arm splintered and drifted away. Kinsley's eyes were struck with fear, and there was nothing I could do about it. She reached for her missing arm and the sudden movement left a trail of particles in its wake.

"Gran!" Kinsley lunged for the safety of my embrace and all but dissolved into the cloud. "Gran!" she called out, and her voice echoed all around me. I searched and searched, but I couldn't find her. Boldly, I pressed through dimension after dimension, searching for my granddaughter, but she had slipped into a space that even I couldn't penetrate.

I let myself fall back into the void of a brewing storm. Kinsley was no longer there, and her cries were replaced with the low whining that reminded me of the bowels of a ballast howling under the weight of the ship. The place was eerie, and I hated that Kinsley had to see it. That she had to feel the frigid air. I pondered how I could help her. And wondered if I could change the things she saw or felt so that it wasn't such a scary place the next time she visited. Because I knew she'd be back.

Kinsley was very much alive but under the sedation of Propofol—a drug-induced coma. She was in a dimension that few could reach. Though I didn't think it was impossible, I only knew that I hadn't found it yet.

I pushed forward into Easton's world. He and Brooklyn were in the waiting room of the hospital, and Clara and Landon were on their way. I gave them as many green lights as I could. It was the small things, and a traffic light was the least I could do for Clara now. I felt for her as she had already been broken down from losing me. It wasn't fair that she had to deal with this, too.

But I knew that no matter how difficult the struggle may be that she could—and would—push through. And when she did, she would be a stronger version of herself. Her perspective would shift, and she would become her best self. I just had to get her to the other side. And already failing my first mission, doubt swirled through the air as I wondered if I could do much for Clara.

When she and Landon arrived, I sat beside her in the waiting room, and I watched Brooklyn's calculating eyes. Many failed attempts later, Brooklyn finally had her chance to talk to Clara when Landon left to find a restroom.

"Clara, you have to listen to me. I don't have much time," Brooklyn said, looking over her shoulder toward the men's restroom.

"Huh?" Clara groaned.

"It's important, Clara. Focus. Kinsley is going to be alright. It's thirteen days. It's thirteen days of pure hell, but it's thirteen days. You can and you will get through this. And Kinsley will too."

"She will? You know?" Clara focused on Brooklyn. Easton listened in.

"She will. You will hear many terrible things while she is in that coma. Setbacks that will threaten to end you. Don't listen. Please!"

"But she's going to be alright, right?"

"Yes. More than alright. She'll make a full recovery." Brooklyn looked over her shoulder. "And one more thing— your mom is with her. She's not alone," she said.

Easton shifted in his seat.

"She is?" Clara asked, wiping her tears with newfound strength and hope.

Brooklyn looked over her shoulder again as Landon emerged from the restroom. "She is . . ." Brooklyn said, nodding.

Clara took a deep breath, and I felt the relief that washed over her. Brooklyn turned to Easton and grabbed his hand. He forced a smile for her, but I knew he was having a hard time knowing I was with Kinsley but that he couldn't reach me. But what Easton didn't know was that he *could* reach me. It was *I* that couldn't get through to him. Not right away, anyhow.

After a long night in the hospital, I sat on the edge of Kinsley's bed during Easton's first visit with her. She was finally stabilized, and guests were allowed back inside, one at a time. I knew that while he held her hand, he wondered if I was near. He spoke to me, at first, in his mind, and eventually, he did so out loud. I heard it all.

"I know you're there, Beck. I know you're with Kinsley, watching over her. But if you could just give me a sign. Something to let me know. Please," he said, under his breath.

Lights sometimes worked for me, but not here. Not in the hospital, where so many lives depended on the machines that they were hooked up to. I didn't want to tamper with the electricity. I had been experimenting with air but hadn't yet been successful with it. Still, I tried. I sucked in a long, bottomless breath and I pushed it with all the might I had. All the love I could spill, I exhaled. And with all the energy I could move through the veil, I tried with everything I had. Easton's back stiffened, and his eyes fixed. I came in close to see the tiny hairs on the back of his neck standing on end. And I smiled.

"Beck?" Easton whispered. I was so happy I could cry. I wanted to yell at the top of my lungs, *I'm here! I'm here!* But I didn't have a voice. Not one that he could hear. "I can feel you," he said when I didn't answer. It was like music to my ears, and I smiled, knowing that I was able to let him know that I was alright.

Over the next thirteen days, I lived in the hospital. I searched for Kinsley in the other dimensions, near and far, and I frequented the last place I had made contact with her. I spent time there, in the void, reciting the stories I had read to her as a child. Folklore and fairytales. And I told her stories I thought she might enjoy now as an adult. And occasionally, she resurfaced.

I'd come to realize that our connection was based on the depth of her drugs. When the doctors lightened her dosage to run various tests . . . that's when I could reach her. I did what I could to cloak the void in which we had our brief meetings, and I believed it worked. I couldn't control the sounds or the temperature that she experienced—it was always far too cold—but I managed to turn the dark thunderous void into a comfortable place.

And on the few occasions that we met, I'd tell her to fight. I'd encourage her to be strong, and I'd let her know we were all rooting for her. I tried to show her the way out, but it was beyond our control. I counted down the days. Our time was always short, but I treasured the brief moments I had with my granddaughter. And it made me a little sad that when she'd wake up, I'd no longer get to visit her.

After thirteen days, when she was brought out of her coma, we celebrated. Kinsley still had a long time to get back to her full self, but we cheered her on every step of the way. And one day, months down the road, Kinsley told Easton of her visits with me while in the hospital.

CHAPTER 28

*T*hree years had passed. Some days were harder than others, but I was there for all of them, nonetheless. Easton had aged more rapidly in my absence, and the girls were worried about him. They took turns visiting and then had long talks on the phone about the funny and sometimes absurd things he would say. But I knew Easton was living out his seniority in a way he never let himself do before. And I think there was a part of him that liked it. Not the brittle bones or the lonely home, but the lack of responsibility that came with being in his old age.

Easton would eat cereal for dinner if he wanted to. He wouldn't get dressed some weeks until Wednesday rolled around—because that's the day one of the girls would come to check on him. And he would spend countless hours putting together the most difficult puzzles or playing solitaire across the dining table. Some nights, he would watch old cop movies and laugh out loud while he remembered his time as a police officer. I'd laugh, too.

But today was a big day for Easton. He had pants on for starters, and he was on his way to Clover's historical chapel. I pulled at his bow tie in the back of the cab. I couldn't straighten it, but I never let myself stop trying. It made me feel involved. I could have skipped time. I could have appeared at the wedding for all the good parts. I didn't. I took the cab. Because I didn't want to be there for just the good parts. I wanted to be there for every stride, big or small.

We got to the chapel with plenty of time to spare. Nora was there early with a handsome man on her arm. She looked stunning, as always, in a fitted navy dress. Happy too. "Hey Dad, how are you feeling today?" Nora asked as she hugged Easton.

"I'm good. How are you? Is this Beau?" Easton asked.

"Hello sir," Beau reached for Easton's hand. I could tell that Easton liked him. Nora did, too. But he wasn't the one. Beau was, however, the first one to stay for a while, and the first one to teach Nora balance. But ultimately, he'd just be the first one who got away. And there would be many after him.

"Let's go get a seat." Nora led the way into the small chapel. Stained glass windows lined each side of the walls, and white ribbon bows dressed the pews. It was simple. Classic.

"So, I hear you play golf? Is that right?" Easton asked Beau as they took their seats in the front row.

"Dad . . ." Nora sighed.

"That's right. Do you play, sir?"

"No. I never spent my time chasing balls."

"Dad!" Nora glared at Easton. Beau chuckled. And I did too.

"What? I didn't," Easton grumbled.

"That's alright. What do you do for fun, then?" Beau asked Easton.

"Well, now, not much. But in my day, I chased the bad guys."

Nora leaned over to Beau. "He means, he was a police officer," she said.

"Oh, wow. I bet you have some crazy stories then?" Beau asked.

"I do!"

"Did you ever get shot?"

"I did!" Easton started to pull at his bow tie.

"Dad! Keep your clothes on! Beau doesn't want to see your bullet hole!" Nora said, her hand over Easton's.

Clara and Landon walked in like a breath of fresh air. Clara wore a yellow sundress and brown leather sandals. She smiled warmly and hugged everyone, including Beau, who she'd just met for the first time. When Beau took his seat, Easton leaned in and said, "You know, I've never been this old before?"

Beau stared at him with empty eyes, and I threw my head back, laughing. Sure, it sounded odd, but it was true. He hadn't let himself get that old before. This was new to him.

"Is that so?" Beau asked, head cocked.

Soon after, Clara's kids came in. Though they were

anything but kids. Kinsley's arm interlocked with her boyfriend's, and her little brother, Conrad—who was now tallest in the family—was with his girlfriend. A bubbly, bright personality that reminded me of Chloe. They were all nice kids and genuinely happy to be at the chapel. They sat on the same side of the church, huddled together, chatting amongst themselves when Tanner came out from behind a curtain with the minister.

They spoke briefly before Tanner took his place on stage, giving Easton a brief, nervous smile. The music started—not the traditional wedding march, but a soft romantic symphony. And our small group stood and turned their attention to the back door, but I couldn't wait.

Brooklyn, dressed in white, stood on the other side of the church doors, her hand frozen on the doorknob. It was a sight I'd wanted to see my whole life. However, I was thrilled I could see it now in the afterlife. I had a better view from here anyhow. More beautiful than Brooklyn's hair or her dress was her heart, which she opened up just enough for Tanner to find his way back into. Still, she stood frozen with trepidation.

Tanner and Brooklyn had been together since I passed away. Tanner would drive to Brooklyn's place every single morning to have coffee and do crossword puzzles with her. Then, they would take a leisurely walk around the neighborhood. It had been that way for so long that the driving to and from no longer made any sense. The only thing that would change after they married in their seventies was that Tanner would spend evenings with

Brooklyn, too. And when they went to bed as early as they did, it really meant just sharing dinner.

Still, Brooklyn was afraid. She'd always worried that marriage would steal her immortality. I placed my hand on top of hers. I whispered in her ear that I loved her and I told her congratulations. She didn't feel my hand on top of hers, and she didn't hear my voice in her ear. But she did find the courage to open the door. She walked into the church with her head held high. And since her parents were long gone, I walked beside her. And it was I who gave her away to Tanner.

Easton cried throughout the ceremony, and when Clara placed her hand on his shoulder, he told her he had something in his eye. But I knew he was thinking of me, because I was thinking of him and the time we wed in the barn. There was a time when Easton only felt sorrow, and while he was on the brink of looking back at our lives together with nothing but fondness, he wasn't there yet. This was a bitter-sweet moment for him.

After dinner, Beau extended his hand to Nora for a dance. I pushed her out of her seat, chanting, "Do it! Do it!" She blushed while taking his hand. Beau pulled her close, gripping Nora's waist and down the small of her back. They danced slowly as she looked into his eyes. If I hadn't known any better, I'd say she was falling for him. But I did know better, and it would stop there. But tonight was the height of the relationship. She was happy and so was he.

"Well, Brooklyn, you did it. You finally did it," Easton said, alone at a table with the bride.

"I finally did. It took some time to get here, but I'm glad

I did. I've always had a soft spot for your brother." Brooklyn took a sip of champagne. The golden liquid shook with the tremors of her hand.

"Yeah. He's never given up on you, that's for sure . . . except—"

"—Except for that one time?" Brooklyn chuckled.

"Yeah, that one time he married someone else. That was just a moment of weakness, though," Easton said with a laugh.

"Look at him, dancing with Clara." Brooklyn pointed a finger at Tanner on the dance floor. It was surely a sight to behold, but the best part was the sound Clara made when she laughed at her uncle Tanner.

"Let me get some of that?" Easton reached for Brooklyn's champagne.

"I thought you weren't supposed to drink with the medication you're on?" she asked.

"Oh, it's just a little bit. It won't kill me. And if it does?" he shrugged with a sly smile on his face. I shook my head. "So what's next for you?" Easton asked Brooklyn.

"Bed! It's way past my bedtime!" Brooklyn said.

"No, I mean, what comes after this life now that you've married?"

"Oh, that. I don't think this will change my path. My fulfillment has always been helping people get where they need to go, and I have more of that to do in the next life. Maybe the next several. I may be here for a while . . ." Brooklyn said as she gazed at Nora, who danced with Beau across the room in a dark corner. He had her hair wrapped around his finger, and she wore a flirty smile.

"You're going to watch out for my girl?" Easton finished the flute of champagne.

"You know I am," she said.

"Good. Good." Easton watched Nora with worry in his eyes.

Tanner came up to Brooklyn, sweaty and excited. "I love this woman!" he said to Easton before he kissed her on the cheek.

"I love you, too, hubby," she said.

"I'm going to run to the restroom. Do you need anything from the bar when I come back?"

Brooklyn looked at her empty champagne glass and then at Easton. "No, thank you," she said.

Tanner danced off, and with him left the fun-loving energy that he had always brought to the table. "I miss her," Easton said. And it was so fast that it was almost automatic. Like he had no control over the confession he spilled.

"*It's not your time,*" I said.

"I know you do. We all do," Brooklyn said.

"Have you had any dreams?"

"Not since the last time you asked," she said with a teasing smile. He'd asked two hours ago.

"I've felt her near. I know she's there. Sometimes I get a cool breeze on my arm or hand—" Brooklyn looked down to the hand I had touched outside of the chapel, and she smiled. "And sometimes I hear her voice. 'I'm here,' she'll say," he said in a whisper.

I watched his eyes turn from dry to moist as I thought of all the times that I'd wanted to scream it. *I'm here!* I said it to him all the time. I had no way of knowing which of them he had heard, but all that mattered was that he knew. He knew that I hadn't left him. "But it's never enough. I think, perhaps, I'm going crazy. She doesn't visit like all my loved ones before, and I worry that something's wrong. Like maybe I've made it all up, and she's out there again."

"You think she came back?" Brooklyn asked.

"I don't know. She could have."

"No. No. No. She didn't come back. I would have known. Trust me, her case is closed. She made it to the other side . . . unless—"

"Unless what?"

"Well, unless, she's here. With you," she said.

"Could that happen?" he asked.

"Yeah, if she's stubborn enough," she said.

Easton smiled. "Then she's here," he said, as a matter of fact.

"I have a feeling she may be keeping an eye out for you. Making sure you don't mix your medications and whatnot."

"Yeah. You're probably right. She's probably here now," he said.

"Probably." Brooklyn looked around for me. But I was right by Easton, and her eyes moved swiftly through my path. "What do you think she'd be doing if she were here now?" she asked.

Easton chuckled. "Dancing. She'd be dancing." I smiled.

"Well then. Shall we?" Brooklyn asked. A wicked smile split across Easton's face and the two of them slowly made their way to the dance floor. I trailed behind them with ease. Easton, though stiff in his old age, still had moves, and he didn't hold any of them back. He danced as if I were there. But this time, I think he believed I was. Tanner came to dance with his bride and soon everyone was on their feet. I drifted back and forth like a deep-ocean current.

When the night was over and Easton lay on our bed alone, he fell asleep with peace in his heart. It was the first time since my passing that the light had crept in. The chapter had finally come to an end where his despair ruled all else. And I looked forward to the next eight years Easton had left. Even though I'd be invisible to him, I was patient. More than I'd ever been capable of before. Death did that to you.

When time was no measure of currency, impatience ceased to exist. And it only made me happy to know that he was living again. Even in my absence, the next eight years would be some of his happiest times. And I wouldn't miss it for the world. I'd be the sunlight that shined down on him on a warm summer day, and I'd be the crackle in the fire that hypnotized him on a cool fall evening. I'd be there by his side until the day that he was there by mine.

uburn and mustard leaves masked the bluffs eight times over. Easton's time was running out like the sand in an hourglass. He had made several new friends over the years. And getting dressed only one day a week became a thing of the past. He kept a busy schedule, and on most nights, he was in bed by seven, resting for his next full day. Time flew by, not only for him but for me, too.

While Easton filled his days the best he knew how, I tinkered with electricity, tampered with dreams, moved small objects, and sent dragonflies, butterflies, and songbirds on paths to a smile. I danced by myself in the shadows of our dark home. And when it rained, I would scale high above the clouds and wait for the first sign of a rainbow to paint the sky. I'd watch until the world below was covered in the ethereal glow, and I'd imagine it was art.

Easton joined the police department's volunteer group and would sometimes drive around in a police car. His favorite was talking to the new cops that were just starting out, both eager and afraid. He'd tell them all the things he'd learned over the years. In the weeks that Easton didn't volunteer, he would meet up with other retired cops in the program and often hosted a poker night at the house.

Poker nights were the best. The men would complain about many things. The pills their doctor put them on. Their aches and pains. How they couldn't do this or that any longer. But when they complained about their wives—their old ladies—Easton would fall quiet. I knew he'd give anything for the chance to complain alongside his buddies, but I was no longer around to annoy him, and he'd all but forgotten the ways I used to drive him crazy.

They were a funny group of men, though, and I enjoyed listening to their stories about past jobs they'd been on and the crazy things they'd seen. I'd play with the cigar smoke that rose underneath the dining room light and I'd try to manipulate it in ways that could get someone's attention. Practice for later, when Easton was alone. But he never smoked cigars alone. Not until the day he became a great-grandpa.

When Kinsley had her first baby, Easton smoked a celebratory cigar with her husband. I tried to manipulate the smoke, but only once did I think that maybe Easton had seen it. Something in the way his eyes focused and his brows knitted made me think he saw me etched in the smooth lines of his cigar smoke like a charcoal drawing. I felt his heart pick up speed, but if it were true and he had seen me, he said nothing to allude to it.

On the days that Easton spent holding his great-grandson, he was the happiest. The baby boy would sleep in his arms, and Easton would just watch. I watched too, and I couldn't have been prouder of Kinsley and the family she made for herself. Sometimes, when she rocked her baby to sleep, she'd read the old books I bought for her when she was born. They were torn and tattered now, but that only meant they were well-loved. It didn't take long before she became pregnant again, and I had a feeling that one day she would have a large, boisterous family.

When all the poker games and police volunteer work had become far and few in between, I could feel that Easton's heart had weakened, and I could see that a marked tiredness had taken over his body. He still wanted to do all the things he had done before, but getting up to do anything made him short of breath. And one day, I caught him writing in a journal that I'd never seen before.

I peered over his shoulder, surprised to see my name at the top of the page. He wasn't writing goodbye letters to the girls like I had—but a love letter to me. He wrote slowly, concentrating on his penmanship. He talked to me like I was still alive. He told me how much he missed me. How much he had seen me in everything he did. He told me how much I had missed. About our great-grandson, about Nora's firm, and Clara's emerging passion for pottery. He told me how he missed my tattoo and how sometimes he'd still laugh at the funny things I did. Or at how mad I got when I lost a bet.

But what he wrote next I couldn't pry my eyes from. And my focus lingered there for some time.

I'll be seeing you soon.

Easton stared at his love letter—my love letter. And I studied the last line. When he was satisfied, he folded it up and left it on his desk. Then, he slipped on an olive button-down sweater and his brown leather loafers and left the house. A cab showed up at the door, and when I saw he had directed the cab driver to the grocery store, I deemed it safe to leave him to grocery shop while I answered the call I had from Nora.

Nora sat on a blanket by my grave at the cemetery. A single tear rolled down her cheek as she picked petals one by one out of a pink rosebud. She missed me. And she was having a hard time. I ran my hands through the grass and listened to her talk about her struggles. I tried to pull the stress out of her, but it was something that she would have to do on her own. I only had the power to be there for her, but even that had gone unnoticed.

Nora didn't come to the cemetery often. None of them did anymore. But today there weren't only roses from Nora, but sunflowers from Brooklyn, too. On days like today—a special occasion—there would be more visits to the gravesite. But they never needed to come here to see me or show me their love. I always felt it. Every time a memory would spark warmth in their hearts or they'd wake from a dream of me. Any time my name left their mouths—it was just like them bringing flowers to my grave. I felt their affection all the same.

When Nora's eyes dried and she fell silent, I told her about Easton. I told her how he wrote me the sweetest letter. How he said he'd see me soon. And how I felt excited for the first time in a while—like I had a date coming up. I hadn't been on a date in years. When she said goodbye, I said goodbye to the grave too. Because I was coming with her, not staying. Nora climbed into her luxury sports coupe, and while I loved riding in it with the top down, I knew she was headed to the house to see Easton, and I wanted to beat her there.

But when I came to the house, something was off. Something was different. I didn't sense Easton at first, like I usually would have. My tether seemed to have slackened, and I found myself unsure of where I belonged. I went to the desk where he had left my love letter, and beside it was a grand bouquet of red roses adorned with wooden twine and baby's breath. A note stuck out from roses with a simple note saying.

Happy Anniversary, my love.

I glanced around the empty room, listening for the drum of Easton's heart. And it was in the silence that I remembered our plan. The only plan we had ever made in case of an emergency. I looked at the calendar pinned to the wall above Easton's desk. May 7 circled with a red heart. It was all I needed to be on my way. I fled the house, catching a glimpse of brown leather loafers sprawled across the kitchen floor and Nora's sports car pulling into the driveway on my way out. It all happened in a blur as I hurried to our spot. It was there that time stopped completely.

A silhouette stood in the middle of the road on the New River Bridge. Even though I didn't recognize the figure in the distance, I didn't need my eyes to trust that my heart had found its counterpart. He turned, taking in his surroundings, and I lost my stomach as I imagined he was looking for me. But I wasn't sure that he could see me. I'd been invisible for so long.

I caught the sunlight that lit the side of Easton's face, and when it lit his glacier eyes to a shade of blue that I'd never seen before, I knew that there was nothing standing in our way. Not time, not dimension, not even fate could touch us now. His eyes drew upon mine with the pull of two magnets, and the corners of his lips pulled into a flirty smile. I made my way to him slowly. His face youthful as I approached him. Easton looked just like the day I'd met him, only this time, he was strong, proud, and happy.

I stopped just before him. His hair lifting in the gentle breeze. "You found me," I said.

He smiled. "I knew just where to look." He looked over me, his smile never fading. "I'm sorry I kept you waiting."

"It wasn't long at all," I said.

"You look young. Like when I met you, but healthy, strong."

"It feels that way, doesn't it?" I asked.

"Yeah. It does," Easton said as he looked at the back of his smooth hands, not a wrinkle or age spot to be found. I took his hands and slowly, ever so slowly, lifted onto my toes and planted a feather-light kiss upon his lips.

When I pulled away, he stared in wonder. "I can't believe I found you . . ."

"I knew you would," I said, taking his hand and leading him down the middle of the bridge.

"So, what do we do now?" he asked, looking around as if seeing the world for the very first time.

I threw my head back, laughing. "Just wait, it's only the beginning . . ."

Thank you for taking the time to read The Tethered Soul Series. It means the world to me.

Please take a moment to write a review, it really makes my day!

For more information, subscribe here:

https://www.subscribepage.com/redenbooks
Xoxo,
Laura

ABOUT THE AUTHOR

Laura C. Reden is an emerging author who likes to add paranormal and fantasy twists while tugging at the heart strings.

Overcoming the struggles of dyslexia, Laura found that creative passion and hard work triumphs over her disadvantage.

Laura is a Southern Californian native, wife, and mother of two daughters. Her pastimes include video production, pottery, and horseback riding. While she received an education in social and behavioral science, she currently works as the chief financial officer for her family-owned law firm in San Diego.

If you are interested in staying updated on new releases, subscribe to my monthly email list. It's short and sweet with opportunities to help name characters, get advanced review copies, and even have your pet featured in upcoming scenes.

https://www.subscribepage.com/redenbooks

Xoxo,

Laura

ALSO BY

THE TETHERED SOUL SERIES

LAURA C. REDEN

DREAMS ARE FICKLE, EMOTIONS ARE BOLD.

THE
PHANTOM SERIES

CAUGHT BETWEEN WORLDS,
KINSLEY WILDE CAN SEE THE DEAD,
MANIFEST HER DREAMS, AND CONJURE HER FEARS.

NOTES FOR BOOK CLUB:

NOTES FOR BOOK CLUB:

www.ingramcontent.com/pod-product-compliance
Lightning Source LLC
Chambersburg PA
CBHW061057190726
48286CB00006B/1788